## "Hello, Katherine."

That deep, dangerous voice…

The humidity closed in despite the air-conditioning and cut off the words in Kate's throat. Sweat beaded at her temple and on the back of her neck. He was still the best-looking man she'd ever seen.

"I, uh," she stammered. Taking a deep breath, she lifted her chin. "Hello, Chase. You took me by surprise. It's been a long time. How've you been?"

"Considerably better than last time we saw each other, *chère*."

"All right, Chase. What do you want here?"

It took a few seconds for him to answer. She couldn't breathe.

"Everything, Kate," he finally told her. "I want it all."

Dear Reader,

Sit back, relax and indulge yourself with all the fabulous offerings from Silhouette Desire this October. Roxanne St. Claire is penning the latest DYNASTIES: THE ASHTONS with *The Highest Bidder.* Youngest Ashton sibling, Paige, finds herself participating in a bachelorette auction and being "won" by a sexy stranger. Strangers also make great protectors, as demonstrated by Annette Broadrick in *Danger Becomes You,* her most recent CRENSHAWS OF TEXAS title.

Speaking of protectors, Michelle Celmer's heroine in *Round-the-Clock Temptation* gets a bodyguard of her very own: a member of the TEXAS CATTLEMAN'S CLUB. Linda Conrad wraps up her miniseries THE GYPSY INHERITANCE with *A Scandalous Melody.* Will this mysterious music box bring together two lonely hearts? For something a little darker, why not try *Secret Nights at Nine Oaks* by Amy J. Fetzer? A handsome recluse, an antebellum mansion—two great reasons to stay indoors. And be sure to catch Heidi Betts's *When the Lights Go Down,* the story of a plain-Jane librarian out to make some serious changes in her humdrum love life.

As you can see, Silhouette Desire has lots of great stories for you to enjoy. So spend this first month of autumn cuddled up with a good book—and come back next month for even more fabulous reads.

Enjoy!

*Melissa Jeglinski*

Melissa Jeglinski
Senior Editor
Silhouette Desire

Please address questions and book requests to:
Silhouette Reader Service
U.S.: 3010 Walden Ave., P.O. Box 1325, Buffalo, NY 14269
Canadian: P.O. Box 609, Fort Erie, Ont. L2A 5X3

# A SCANDALOUS MELODY
## LINDA CONRAD

*Silhouette*
# Desire

Published by Silhouette Books

**America's Publisher of Contemporary Romance**

SILHOUETTE BOOKS

ISBN 0-373-76684-X

A SCANDALOUS MELODY

Copyright © 2005 by Linda Lucas Sankpill

This edition published by arrangement with Harlequin Books S.A.

® and TM are trademarks of Harlequin Books S.A., used under license. Trademarks indicated with ® are registered in the United States Patent and Trademark Office, the Canadian Trade Marks Office and in other countries.

Visit Silhouette Books at www.eHarlequin.com

Printed in U.S.A.

**Books by Linda Conrad**

Silhouette Desire

*The Cowboy's Baby Surprise* #1446
*Desperado Dad* #1458
*Secrets, Lies...and Passion* #1470
*\*The Gentrys: Cinco* #1508
*\*The Gentrys: Abby* #1516
*\*The Gentrys: Cal* #1524
*Slow Dancing with a Texan* #1577
*The Laws of Passion* #1609
*Between Strangers* #1619
*†Seduction by the Book* #1673
*†Reflected Pleasures* #1679
*†A Scandalous Melody* #1684

*The Gentrys
†The Gypsy Inheritance

## LINDA CONRAD

Award-winning author Linda Conrad was first inspired by her mother, who gave her a deep love of storytelling. "Actually, Mom told me I was the best liar she ever knew. And that's saying something for a woman with an Irish-storyteller's background," Linda says. In her past life Linda was a stockbroker and certified financial planner, but she has been writing contemporary romances for six years now. Linda's passions are her husband, her cat, Sam, and finding time to read cozy mysteries and emotional love stories. She says, "Living with passion makes everything worthwhile." Visit Linda's Web site at www.LindaConrad.com or write to her at P.O. Box 9269, Tavernier, FL 33070.

This is for my niece, Christine Norris,
a most terrific wife, mom, sister and friend!
Thanks for all your support!

# Prologue

**D**ark, dangerous street corners and after-hours sounds of jazzy blues playing eerily in the distance meant nothing to Passionata Chagari.

She stood quietly in the shadows, awaiting the arrival of the lost heir to the gypsy legacy, Chase Severin. His grandmother, Lucille Steele, was long buried in her grave. Yet just today, Chase had been informed of his status as heir to her fortune.

Now, after a long night of revelry, Chase would receive a bequest that was much more valuable than all of Lucille's money. Passionata patted the deep pocket in the long, flowing silk of her favorite scarlet dress and smiled.

This young man would be the most difficult one to help, she knew. Yet Passionata had given her father her word. No matter what the circumstances, the lost Steele heir was to receive the gift that was meant for him.

Chase Severin wandered out of the French Quarter bar right at closing, mulling over the events of the last couple of days and feeling staggered by everything he'd learned—and perhaps by that last straight shot of bourbon.

He wasn't just the wayward son of a small-town drunk as he'd believed for all of his life. Son of a—

He had actual relatives and shared family trees. And on top of the new fortune, Chase had also inherited an exalted social standing.

Stopping at an empty street corner, Chase lit up one of his long thin cigars and blew a fragrant, gray circle of smoke out into the darkness. He'd meant to quit this nasty habit, and had cut way down. But just now he needed all the help he could get.

His whole life…everything he'd ever believed about himself…most of it simply wasn't true. The secrets and the misunderstandings were still not all clear to him. But he knew things would be different from now on.

Still cloaked by the darkness, Passionata read his mind. She chuckled at the thought of just how truly different this young man's life was about to become.

"Celebrating, Severin?" she said aloud as she stepped into the yellow lamplight. "You have reason."

Chase nearly choked on his own smoke when the strange and creaky voice came unexpectedly out of the shadows. He turned to face one of the oddest women he'd ever seen. She was dressed up in wild colors like a fortune-telling gypsy. The hair that hung loose beneath a deep-purple head scarf was a mottled salt-and-pepper color. And her watery eyes gleamed strangely bright under the streetlight.

"Do we know each other?" he asked when he found his voice.

"I am Passionata Chagari, and I have a debt to repay."

"Not to me, you don't. I keep careful records of my accounts." Chase took a long, thoughtful drag and flipped the cigar in the gutter.

She smiled a partially toothless grin. "This debt is to be repaid in the form of a legacy left to you by your grandmother Steele and by my father, the king of the gypsies."

Most of what she'd said was too weird for Chase to fathom. He'd only been aware of his grandmother Steele's existence for a few days, and the only reason he knew now was because she'd died and left him part of her fortune.

So he took the old woman's arm and held her close. "Don't play with a player, Passionata," he whispered hoarsely. "You'll only lose. What exactly do you want?"

"Your grandmother Steele was a great lady. She would not care for you to treat your elders with such disdain." The old woman pulled her arm from his grip. "Lucille Steele saved my life, the life of my family. She was kind to strangers when no other would take the time."

"I didn't know her," Chase muttered. "But I'm glad to hear you thought she was a good person. Lucille's dead now. Do you expect me to take up your care where she left off?"

The gypsy smiled. "Ever the gambler, Severin? You take the risk now that I may have something of value you need."

She tilted her head to study him and continued. "You

have the chance to change your ways—go back—make right the wrongs. Do you consider the possibilities? Or do you shirk your fate?"

How could she know what he'd been thinking? The moment he'd found out that he'd come from prominent and respectable people, he'd wondered what it would be like to go back.

Passionata reached into a pocket and pulled out something shiny. "This is your part of the gypsy's legacy. It is one of the gifts from my father to the blood descendants of Lucille Steele, in repayment for a kindness."

Chase took the object from her hand and turned it over to study. A golden replica of an egg, the beautiful artifact had a jewel-encrusted design reminiscent of the great Russian artisans. Old and obviously expensive, it looked like something that should've belonged to a king.

"It is old," the gypsy began as if to answer his thoughts. "But it belongs to you, and was made for you alone."

"I'm not that old." He tried to get her to take it back but she stepped away.

"This orb of jewels is crafted to bring everything you've ever wanted, at long last," she told him. "Take it back to the beginning. Keep the magic close and let it give to you the riches that have become your heart's desire."

Chase stared down, mesmerized by the sparkling colors of the precious stones placed in the golden egg-shaped setting. With his new inheritance and the money he'd made from the casinos and the other businesses he'd bought and sold over the years, he could easily afford to buy his own jewels.

But if this was something that should be his heritage… Well, it would be a thing to be proud of. Something to take back and hold out to show that he was a somebody.

"Tell me the whole story of what my grandmother did for your family," he said as he dragged his gaze from the egg.

But the old gypsy woman was gone, and he was once again standing on a deserted street corner—all alone.

# One

"**Y**ou won't believe who's back in town."

Her secretary's words should not have caused a shiver to run along Kate's nerve endings. After all, there were many people who could've come back to Bayou City. But Kate Beltrane knew instinctively who it was that had finally come home.

"I don't have time to guess, Rose. Tell me." She said the words with a small shrug, as if she didn't care. As if the chance to see him again wasn't the one thing she'd dreamed about every day for the past ten years.

"Chase Severin," Rose said in a whisper. "I was only twelve when he left. But I remember him as one juicy hunk of a guy. All the girls had such a crush on him." She fanned herself, acting as if the very thought of him had made her hot and sweaty all of a sudden. "I wonder why he's come home now? His father left town nearly five years ago. He doesn't have any family here anymore."

"How do you know it's him? Did you see him?"

"Mrs. Seville told Sallie Jenkins he checked in to the B&B this morning. The word's all over town."

Kate looked up from her work and noticed that Rose was eyeing her carefully, waiting for some kind of reaction. "We don't have time for gossip," she told Rose in a mild tone.

She knew the old rumors about her and Chase were bound to resurface now that he was back in town. "Lunchtime is over," Kate continued. "And we still have a lot to do if we're going to be ready for our appointment with the new owner of the mill this afternoon.

"I don't suppose Mrs. Seville mentioned anything about a stranger checking in, did she?" she asked Rose, trying to deflect any more conversation about Chase Severin.

Rose shook her head, pulled her reading glasses up from their spot on a chain around her neck and placed them on the bridge of her nose. "No. But maybe the new owner will come here first and then check in there after the meeting."

Seville's B&B was the only place in town for visitors to stay. People did sometimes drive down from one of the motels in New Iberia, and even the hotels of New Orleans were not all that far away. But if a person had business in town, or if they'd come to do a little fishing in the Gulf of Mexico, the deluxe accommodations of the bed and breakfast would be the one and only spot to overnight.

Kate wondered which one had brought Chase back home after all these years. But she didn't have time to dwell on him right now. Getting these files straightened out for the new mill owner was much more urgent.

Later, in the deep dark stillness of night when the wind whipped through moss-covered live oaks and alligators stealthily slipped through coffee-colored waters hunting for a meal... Later, in the same quiet and sleepless hour of the night that had become Kate's constant and dearest companion... Later. That's when she would take the time to guess about him...and to remember.

"Go back to work, Rose," she said with a heavy heart. "We only have a couple more hours before we can stop guessing. When the man gets here, we'll know for sure."

Two hours after her discussion with Rose, Kate took a minute to pin up a few loose strands of her unruly curls, readying herself for the appointment. She'd tried hard over the past few years to dress in a more business-like manner. It wasn't in her nature to wear dress suits. She was a bayou girl at heart. And any shoe with closed toes was not to her taste.

But recently she'd begun to feel as if she owed it to her father—no, check that. She owed it to the town and its dependence on this mill—to look professional.

In a matter of days, the mill could be shut down for good. And with it would go the history, dreams and hopes of every one of Bayou City's twelve hundred residents.

With a quiet sigh, Kate smoothed her hair and inspected the stacks of files on the desk before her. She'd done her best.

The man who would arrive today was from the corporation that had bought the mill. He would be the one to make the final decision about whether this mill could be put into a good enough position to emerge from bankruptcy, or if the place should be torn down. The future of the mill and the town was out of her hands.

Not that it had ever really been up to her, anyway. No, her father had seen to that.

And to top off a truly miserable day, Chase had come back to town. It figured that he would choose one of her worst moments to show up.

After all this time, it was hard to imagine that he was actually close enough for her to feel his presence. She'd waited so long to see him again.

If she closed her eyes, she could still hear his laughter after ten years. She could still experience the low, rough rumble of his sensual whispers as he'd spoken to her of love on that wonderful June night so long ago.

The most wonderful and the most horrible night of her entire life.

Kate swallowed hard and opened her eyes. Positive Chase's reason for coming home had nothing to do with seeing her, she nevertheless still longed for just a glimpse of him.

It would be better for both of them if they didn't have to face each other—face the hard truths of their shared past. But she would give her right arm for one last look into the quiet gray eyes of the man she had loved since she was ten years old.

Kate heard the anterior reception door open as Rose spoke softly to whomever had just arrived. So…the new owner of the mill was a few minutes early for his appointment. The man must be eager to begin dismantling what little was left of her ancestors' dreams.

Curious, Kate stood and moved to the partially open

door between her office and Rose's. Maybe she could catch a glimpse of the corporation's man and try to judge his intentions from his looks.

She peeked through the crack, and had to twist around so she could see past Rose's desk to find the stranger. Over her secretary's shoulder, Kate caught her first view of the man she had been expecting.

But with a soft gasp, she froze. It wasn't her appointment. No, just to devil her today—just to make her life more of a living hell than it had been for the last ten years—it was Chase Severin, live and very much in the flesh.

He was talking to Rose and smiling down at the secretary with the same boyish grin that had driven Kate wild as a girl. It wasn't the boy that she saw now, but a man. A man dressed in a blue blazer and tan slacks, who looked somehow taller, broader and sexier than the eighteen-year-old of her dreams.

Sudden erotic flashbacks of scraping her nails against that broad back, of dragging her fingers through the hair on his chest while he pleasured her lips—and all those other more delicate places—drove a deep breathtaking ache through her body.

Not now. Please don't come around to make me lose my mind today, Chase. Not today of all days, when I'm trying to stay so strong.

Her back to Kate, Rose started to get up from her desk. Just as suddenly Chase raised his eyes to Kate's office door and for one crazy moment his gaze met hers. Kate's hands trembled at the sight of the dark-gray eyes that she hadn't forgotten for one day in the past ten years.

He was still the best-looking guy she'd ever seen. Only even better as a grown man. With a monumental effort, she turned and scurried back to her desk. Chase was coming her way, there didn't seem to be anything she could do to stop him. The door swung wide just as she reached her chair and turned around.

"You won't believe this," Rose said as she came into the office with Chase right on her heels. "You remember Chase Severin, don't you, Kate? Well, he's the man we've been expecting. Isn't that a surprise?"

"What...?" *Surprise* was hardly the word for all the emotions that were shooting through her mind and body at the moment. Confusion mixed with remembered desire and caused chaos in her mind.

"Hello, Katherine," he said in that deep, dangerous voice she had heard so often in the wind and in the rain.

The Louisiana humidity, the nasty low-down kind that usually never bothered her, closed in despite the air-conditioning and cut off the words in Kate's throat. Sweat beaded at her temple and on the back of her neck and she couldn't think of what to say.

He narrowed his eyes. "I guess if a person doesn't say goodbye, that must make it okay for them to ignore hello. Is that right, Ms. Beltrane?" His bitterness was plain...understandable but still hurtful at the same time.

"I, uh," she stuttered. Taking a deep breath, she lifted her chin. "Hello, Chase. You took me by surprise. I'm sorry. It's been a long time. How've you been?"

"Considerably better than I was the last time we saw each other, *chère*."

Okay, Kate admitted to herself. Chase had a right to be angry with her—even after ten years. What she'd done deserved his anger and much more. But she was no longer the scared little *poulette* of her childhood years. Afraid of scandal and rumors, afraid of her father.

"Rose, will you excuse us, please?" she asked her secretary. If this was going to be a rehash of yesteryear, she didn't want the worst of it ending up as gossip around town. There were plenty of other subjects for the citizens to stew about these days.

The secretary excused herself and shut the door behind her. Kate had a momentary flash of fear at being closed up with a man who must hate her guts. But her own curiosity and pride overcame it.

Whatever Chase Severin might be, he would never hurt her physically. She knew that right down to the toes of her too-tight shoes.

"All right, Chase. What do you really want here?"

It took a few long seconds for him to answer. Kate couldn't breathe and wished she'd turned up the air-conditioning earlier. But biting her tongue, she waited.

"Everything, Kate," he finally told her. "I want it all. And this time I'm not leaving before I take what I've got coming…starting with the mill."

She felt the confusion and shock spread across her face and reached a hand out to steady herself against the desk. "The mill is in bankruptcy. A corporation has secured the liens that my father…"

"Your dead father, you mean?" Chase interrupted with a sneer. "The one who not only ran me out of town ten years ago, but who also ran the mill right over the edge into oblivion with his careless management."

"You work for the corporation that has come to take over the operation of the mill?" Kate's knees were knocking together so loudly that she was petrified he would hear and mock her for it.

"I *am* the corporation, Kate. Surprised? I'm the sole owner of the corporation that now owns the mill. And I haven't decided yet whether to continue operations or burn the thing to the ground."

The soft gasp escaped her throat before she had a chance to swallow it down. "You have a right to be angry at my father…and at me. But this mill has always been the lifeblood of the town that raised you. You have no cause to take some kind of fanatic revenge against the whole town."

Chase reached into his jacket pocket and withdrew a slender cigar. Without asking permission, he lit it up and then sat down in her chair while he blew out a fragrant cloud of smoke.

"Don't I?" he asked with a wry grin.

Chase found he could barely breathe as the room began closing in around him. But he would never let her know how he'd been affected. After ten long years, he was close enough to the woman he had loved and lost to actually reach out and touch her face.

The conflicting emotions swelled in his chest. For so long he had wanted revenge. He'd dreamed of it. Tasted it.

Breathed it in along with his air.

It was revenge against Kate's father, Henry Beltrane, that had occupied his mind for all this time, though. And the bastard had gone and died six months ago. Now, Chase suddenly discovered his intentions toward Kate were much more complicated than he had imagined.

He'd set her up today, just to see what kind of reaction she would have to learning he was the one who now had charge of her future. But he hadn't counted on the fact that with one look, she would still be able to stir his soul and weaken his knees with the very same desperate need he'd had for her as a teenager.

Chase let the nicotine soothe his jangled nerves, while he kept his best poker face on for Kate's benefit. This whole scene was like something out of his dreams.

At twenty-seven, she hadn't changed much from the sweet seventeen-year-old wisp of a girl whom he'd poured his heart out to. Her hair was still a wild riot of ebony curls, even though she'd tried to pin them up off her slender neck. That soft white neck he alternately wanted to kiss—and to wring.

Just now, her rich chocolate eyes were every bit as wild as her hair. There was obvious fear in them. Fear of him and the power he now held over her life.

He wasn't too sure he liked seeing those particular emotions from her. Yes, it was what he'd thought he wanted. He'd wanted her—wanted everyone—to pay.

At this moment, however, seeing her again and being this close to the reality of his dreams...it was not fear that he would've chosen to see in her eyes when she looked at him. Sensual awareness and need were what he longed to see—what he'd secretly desired for so many years.

"Sit down, Kate," he said in as steady a voice as he could manage.

Could he find the words to say that he wanted her to realize what she'd thrown away the night she let him leave town? And that he wanted her and the whole town to regret what they had let happen to him that night.

She looked pained, as if he'd struck her, and she put the back of her hand against her lips.

But she just as suddenly turned, opened a file drawer and pulled out an ashtray. "Here. If you must have that nasty thing, you'll need this." Her eyes flashed, dark and furious.

Ah. There was his Kate. The one he remembered from youthful stolen moments and shared secrets. So strong willed. So proud.

He stubbed out the cigar as Kate primly took the secretary's chair opposite him. "Still the proper princess, *chère?* I would've thought ten years and the loss of your father and his fortune might have brought you down to earth with the rest of us mere mortals."

"What I am...what I've become...is not the point. What have *you* become, Chase?" She straightened her spine and sat stiffly at the edge of her chair. "Apparently you have money now. What else is different about you? Will you destroy a whole town just for the hell of it?"

God, how he wanted her. The sudden slashing need to run his hands along her body's curves—her narrow waist, the high-tipped breasts—was so strong it actually made him wince.

He wasn't a womanizer. Never had been. And what with his tight business schedules and his bruised memories of youthful romance, he rarely got involved with women. Certainly a few of them had passed through his nights throughout the years, but they were women who knew he only wanted the pleasure of their company for a short time. That he had nothing else to offer.

His affairs were brief, consensual and devoid of passion.

But this was his Kate. The woman he had hated for ten long years. So the desperate erotic need he'd felt when he looked at her had come as a complete shock.

He'd been anxious to see her face, to see the whole town's collective and astonished face, when they figured out their former whipping boy was the person behind the corporate facade who'd bought out the mill. He'd wanted that revenge. They owed it to him.

But it hadn't occurred to him that he would feel other things beyond satisfaction. Kate had never married, and according to town gossip had never had a lasting serious relationship over the past ten years. Chase figured that must be because she thought she was too good for the men around her, the way she'd apparently felt about him all those years ago.

Cold. Frozen. Man-eater. Those were the words used on the streets of Bayou City to describe his former girlfriend.

But that wasn't what he felt when he looked at her now. No, Chase felt the flames licking at his libido as strongly now as he ever had as a randy teenager.

His conflicted emotions raised the stakes for this game.

"What I decide to do about the mill in the end will be all about business," he finally told her. "It's my deal now, Kate. I hold all the cards."

"I see," she said as she tilted her head to question him. "Then what do you want from me? Am I just to go home and never return to my family's mill again?"

"Not at all, *bébé*." He watched her carefully. "In the first place, I'll need your assistance in going over the mill records and reports and will pay you for that time. I suspect you'll be needing the money.

"And in the second place, you no longer have a house to go home to. I will expect you to pack and be out by the first of the week."

"Live Oak Hall?" Her voice rose three octaves, but her panic didn't thrill him as it should have. "You can't mean…"

"I mean that I own it, or rather I hold the mortgage on it, too. Your father left nothing that wasn't in debt, and I'm calling in your mortgage at the end of the week."

She blinked her eyes and he saw her chin tremble. "I knew the mortgage was behind, but I thought the bank would give me more time. Where will I go? Where will I stay if you kick me out of the plantation that's been my family's home for over a hundred years?"

He felt a niggle of pity stirring in his soul, but he tried to ignore it. "Blame your father for your troubles, not me. Perhaps I'll consider renting you one of the guest cottages. If you can afford it, that is."

Tears welled in her eyes, but instead of crying she set her chin defiantly. This was his time at long last. But now that it had finally arrived, he found that her pain gave him absolutely no satisfaction and her pride turned him on.

And he almost hated her for it.

Almost.

# Two

$\mathbf{A}$ wicked wind blew black storm clouds up from the Gulf and threatened to tear new leaves off the ancient oaks lining the allée drive in front of Live Oak Hall. Standing in the kitchen and looking out the window, Kate knew cold late-spring rains would come in a few more minutes. Right before sunset.

But even with Kate's vivid imagination, she was positive those rains didn't have the power to wash away the sting of memories, the heartbreak of wanting things to be different. Lord, how she had dreamed of having the opportunity to make other choices in her life, to go back in time and change what had happened.

Now that Chase had come home, it was clear that she would have to face some of those old poor choices. He wouldn't let her escape them any longer.

She knew her secrets and her mistakes would eventually come out. But there was one cruel secret that she would never give up. No matter what.

Nothing could ever pry that one from her heart. Not even to save her from Chase's hatred. It had to stay buried. Where it belonged.

"I can't believe Chase Severin owns the mill now." Shelby Rousseau, Kate's oldest and best friend, frowned once then smiled as she captured her toddler daughter and lifted the little girl into her high chair.

"Well, I'm afraid he does, Shell." Kate wasn't sure how to explain the rest of it to the one person who had stuck with her through the worst of times. And far in the back of her mind, Kate still had hope of a reprieve.

Sitting down at her huge kitchen table to watch Shelby finish preparing their supper, Kate agonized over what she knew she had to say. How could she tell her friend that her home was lost? That the young single mother would soon be evicted from the guest cottage where she had been raising her daughter.

That Kate herself would soon be homeless was irritating enough. But to think of throwing out Shelby and her baby…

Her dearest friend made the very best mother Kate had ever known. Shell loved her child enough to do anything, go through anything, to keep her daughter safe and to keep the two of them together.

"Would you please hand Madeleine a cracker to get her by for a few minutes until supper is ready?" Shelby asked as she dipped up the shrimp étouffée from the ancient pot on an even older stove.

Kate reached over and put a cracker into the baby's

hand. The little girl stared up with a big, mostly tooth-less grin on her face.

The toddler's cheeks glowed a rosy, healthy pink. Her curious blue eyes were wide and spoke volumes about how smart she was. Sweet Maddie looked just like her mother. But she made Kate think of another baby from long ago. A baby whose smile Kate would never know.

As much as Kate loved Maddie, it hurt a little bit to be near her. But for today, just like most days, Kate buried the pain.

"How's your catering business coming along?"

Shelby served the étouffée and sat down. "It's been good recently. After I booked that party over in New Iberia, I've had several calls about future engagements." Shelby poured ice tea from the frosty pitcher. "I don't know how great things will be if the mill goes out of business, though."

Instead of picking up her spoon to eat, Shelby laid a hand over Kate's. "I'm most worried about you, *chère*. What will you do if Chase shuts down the mill?"

Good question. But not one Kate was prepared to consider just yet.

She shrugged in answer and tried to steer the conversation in a different direction. "I'm a survivor, Shell. I can do lots of things. I'm only worried about the town. There isn't much else for people to do around here. But maybe Chase will find a way to keep it open."

Hesitating for a second, Kate decided to let her friend in on just a small slice of her fears and questions. "I can't understand why Chase bought out the mill at all. The debt load is tremendous. If he decides to put any money into it, it'll be like throwing the cash down a gator hole."

Shelby smiled at her. "Maybe he bought the mill and came back here because of you. I bet he's still in love with you."

Kate shook her head so hard the curls jumped out of their clip and flew wildly about her face. "Not a chance in hell of that. You didn't see his eyes when he first came into my office this afternoon. There was such...hatred. Such bitterness in them when he looked at me."

"Well, there has to be some reason that he would come back to this poor town," Shelby said as she spooned mashed stew into the baby's mouth. "The rumor mill has it that he's really rich now. Drives a Jaguar. Owns houses in St. Thomas and Vail. Made it all by gambling, they say."

"Don't believe everything you hear."

"Do you know something different? Like how he really made his money?"

"No," Kate mumbled. "But I know the rumors of why he left town in the first place have been a bunch of lies. So why should all the rumors about his return be the truth?"

Shelby wiped her baby's chin and blew on a steaming spoonful of étouffée for herself. "You never did tell me the truth of what happened that night. I've always wondered about it."

"It was a dreadful night. I would've given anything if you'd been here that summer to help me through it instead of off visiting with your *grandmère* in New England." Kate had lost her appetite and gave up the pretense of eating.

Shelby chuckled and then frowned. "I guess I must've missed my chance forever. After ten years you still don't want to talk about it, do you?"

"Not really. But I will tell you that all those stories about Chase being drunk and going nuts are all lies. Every one of them. He was stone sober, and he was forced into that fight with Justin-Roy and those boys."

"I didn't know Chase as well as you did back then," Shelby began quietly. "But I never believed he would drink too much. Not when you'd told me how much he hated the fact that his father was always so drunk."

Tears stinging the back of Kate's eyes threatened to put an early end to the conversation and to supper. "Shelby, you are my best friend. You know I love you and Madeleine, don't you?"

"Of course I do, honey. I know you love *us,* this old run-down plantation, the town…and Chase Severin." Shelby dropped her spoon and hugged her when Kate began to protest that last part. "We love you, too. And Maddie and I appreciate you taking us in and letting me trade house cleaning and cooking for a chance to stay in one of the guest houses. You've been a lifesaver."

Oh, Lord. Kate could not make her mouth say the words. She just could not tell her best friend that their days at Live Oak Hall were numbered.

Maybe if she went to Chase. If she begged him to let Shelby and the baby stay on, he would consider it. It wouldn't be the first time that Kate had gotten down on her knees to plead for something important.

She could only hope that this time would turn out a whole lot better than the last one.

Chase picked up his coffee mug and walked alone out onto the B&B's terrace to watch as the lightning dashed silver streaks across the night sky. He loved the smell of the fresh earth right after a rain.

It had been a long time since he'd been able to breathe in the clean night air and listen to the sounds that the swamp critters made after sundown.

He'd had one hell of a day, coming back to Bayou City and seeing the surprised expressions on the faces of its citizens as he deliberately drove his new XK8 in that flashy topaz color right down Lafayette Street.

He knew the word had spread all over town within minutes. The boy who would never amount to anything was back—and rich. His hand automatically went to the pocket of his navy blazer for a triumphant cigar.

But instead of cigars, Chase's hand landed on the antique jeweled egg that he'd begun to carry with him everywhere. He smiled at the very idea that he owned something so valuable and old. It was unlikely the whole damn town collectively would be able to afford just the insurance on anything this expensive.

Feeling the shimmer of electricity beneath his fingers that reminded him that the gypsy had claimed this egg held magic, he withdrew his hand and shook his head. He didn't need any kind of crutch in order to face his old ghosts, not nicotine nor magic. This time he had control of the deck. His cards had turned up in a royal flush.

And he couldn't be happier to have Kate's fate thrown into the pot. It upped the stakes.

When he'd first had that private investigator research the town to find out what had happened here since he'd been gone, he was disheartened to learn that her father had died of cancer six months earlier. Too late. Chase had made the decision to come back and get even with the old *crotte* Beltrane and the rest of the town too late.

But then he'd learned about the mill's bankruptcy and figured his timing was impeccable. He had been given the perfect opportunity to destroy them all.

"Chase?"

He turned around at the sound of her voice, nearly positive it would just be the ghost that had haunted his nights for what seemed like forever. But it was the real Kate this time, standing there with the lights streaming from the French doors at her back.

"Uh, Madame Seville said it would be all right for me to come out here to talk to you. I'm not catching you at a bad time, am I?"

Her midnight-black curls were pulled back in a loose ponytail and glistened with rain. Drips of water trickled down her porcelain cheeks and clung to her dark, thick lashes. She had a khaki-colored trench coat thrown over her arm, and rainwater was puddling under her as she stood there waiting for him to give her an answer.

The sight of her simply stunned him, took his words away. He reached a hand toward his shirt pocket without thinking, then cursed himself silently for being such a fool. He didn't need help facing this echo of days gone by, despite the fact she was the most gorgeous creature he had ever laid eyes on.

"What are you doing here?" he asked with a forced grin. "I thought we'd agreed to start on the books first thing in the morning?"

"I need to talk to you, Chase." She raised her chin in that smug little way she'd had as a girl and took a tentative step closer.

"Talk? I'll just bet you have a lot to say now." He turned his back on her and spread his feet for the balance he badly needed at the moment. "You're ten years too late. You have nothing to say that I care to hear anymore."

"Please," she whispered from behind him. "This isn't about the mill. I'm hoping that will be strictly business with you. But what I wanted to talk about tonight was…"

"Not about the past, I'd wager." He spun around and glared down at her in the slanted light. "I'd give better than even odds that you'd rather die than have to face your past sins tonight. Am I right?"

She was a good half foot shorter and the shadows cast by the back light kept him from seeing her face clearly. But he did manage to catch the anger in her glinting stare, and he watched her work her slender white throat as she swallowed back a nasty remark.

Tempting, this ghost from his past. Too tempting.

Kate shook her head and straightened her shoulders. "I don't think it would serve any purpose to go over our mistakes at this late date."

Just to please himself, to give in to the urgent need to arouse her, Chase moved closer. She backed up a step and he took another in her direction, deliberately pushing her and limiting her personal space.

"My only mistake was in trusting you once, telling you that I loved you." He heard the evil chuckle coming from his own lips and wondered at just how far he had come away from the naive young kid he had been back then. "It's a mistake I never intend to repeat."

Her eyes closed and he heard her soft sigh. Regrets? From the ice princess, Kate Beltrane?

The silent whiff of her perfume reached icy fingers

into his soul. The smell of camellias and gardenia that he'd once imagined he would never be able to get out of his mind took a swift sledgehammer to his heart.

He felt that soft underbelly of pity and desire creeping up on him again as he reached a hand toward her shoulder. Before he could give her comfort, her eyes popped open and determination narrowed those full tantalizing lips.

"I didn't come here tonight to rehash old wounds," she told him with sudden fervor. "I came to ask…explain really…about Live Oak Hall."

"You came here…in the rain…to explain about that broken-down old plantation?" He allowed himself a sneer, but didn't back away from her.

"It's about the guest cottage. My friend, I don't know if you remember her, Shelby Rousseau?"

When he just squinted at her, Kate rushed ahead. "Well, she's a single mother now and trying to get a business started. And…I've been letting her trade out cleaning and cooking to stay in the guest cottage. She can't afford to pay rent, you see, and I thought…"

"You have to start remembering that Live Oak Hall is mine now." He shook his head and grimaced. "No rent? You must've inherited your father's great business sense."

The humiliation ran through Kate's veins. She couldn't stop it from smarting. But she could hold her place and not let Chase see how badly he was getting to her.

He would have no way of knowing how she had begged and pleaded with her father to let her help make the business decisions for the mill. Two years of business college didn't make her an expert, but she'd seen what a mess he had been making of the fiances. How he'd run off the best customers and overpaid the farmers for their rice in years when crops were plentiful.

But her father had quite typically berated her back then. Reminded her that a girl could not know what was best in business. He'd relegated her to the accounting pool, telling her account books were for females. And if she would ever have the sense to marry, her husband could give the advice while she gave him the grandchildren.

"This isn't about business or revenge," she told Chase with a surprisingly steady voice. "It's about friendship and love. Please…"

Chase took her chin with a firm grip, frightening her at first. Then he leaned close enough that she could hear his ragged breathing and could smell his desire. The man still wanted her. After everything she'd done.

The shock of realization and the breathlessness of staring into his deep-gray eyes kept her silent too long. Chase must've sensed the weakness and moved in.

"Friendship and love, huh? And those are things the poor kid from the bad side of town would know nothing about, is that it?" He inched even closer.

She wanted him to kiss her. They were so close that another centimeter would bring their lips together. Dreams of one more kiss from Chase had kept her going in the darkest hours.

But tonight it wouldn't be the same as in her dreams. Tonight the rage in them both would make it all wrong.

The panic drove her back in time to become once again the ten-year-old girl who'd run away from home and found a scary but perfectly safe shelter with an old drunk and his twelve-year-old son. She'd wanted Chase to kiss her then, too, because he'd been her white knight and savior.

But he hadn't kissed her that night. It wouldn't have been right when they were children—and it wouldn't be right now when they were both so tense.

She reared back out of his grasp and shoved at his arms. The coffee mug he'd been carrying all this time slipped to the granite tile floor and shattered into a million pieces.

"Oh, I'm sorry," she cried as she kneeled to clean up the mess. She quickly gathered up a few broken shards and then looked around for some kind of cloth to wipe up the cold coffee and the tiny silvers.

"Just let it go, Kate." He was kneeling beside her and took her arm. "Are you all right?"

"Huh?" She must be in some kind of desire-filled daze, because she couldn't quite understand his meaning.

He gently pried the broken ceramic from her hand and put it aside. "You're bleeding." His big hand encompassed her smaller one, but with a touch so light it nearly brought tears to her eyes.

"It's nothing." She tried to tug her hand away, but he tenderly turned it over to reveal the jagged cut on her middle finger.

Chase's gaze locked with hers as his hard, glinting concern turned in seconds to pure lustful longing. "You need to stop the bleeding first, then clean the wound."

Turning his attention back to her bloody cut, Chase lifted her hand to his lips and slipped the oozing finger into his mouth before she could stop him.

She heard herself gasp and then moan as the sensation of his tongue and lips on her finger became sensual and demanding. Everything else but the two of them and this minute faded into the background.

But a boom of thunder cracked through the air just then and the skies opened up for one more splash of rain. The sound and the chill dragged her back to the present in a hurry.

She tugged on her hand again, and Chase released her. "I'll have it bandaged when I get home."

He stood and pulled her to her feet. "Come under the terrace cover, Kate. You're getting soaked."

"I won't keep you much longer. It's getting late," she told him as they ran for a drier spot. "But I…I still have to plead with you to let Shelby and her daughter continue to stay in the guest cottage. I don't care about myself. I can find somewhere else to go, but for them…"

Dragging her up close to his body, he leaned down to whisper in her ear so that she could hear him over the noise of the rain. "What's it worth to you, *chère?*"

She stiffened and looked up at him. Their bodies were touching. Sweat, heated rainwater and passion came off them in waves, steaming up the air between them. Coming here tonight had obviously been a big mistake.

But she had to keep trying, for Maddie's sake. "I beg you, Chase. Please just consider it." She looked down between them, away from his demanding gaze. But one look made it clear that her aching breasts were peaked and pushing against her cotton blouse, begging for his touch.

Chase saw it as well and leered down at her. "Ah, yes, *bébé,* I can feel the heat between us, too. Odd isn't it, that an ice princess could flare so easily for a ghost?"

He didn't know? He couldn't just look at her and see that her heart still longed for him and that her body still responded to his with no provocation at all?

Her heart pounded in her chest, but she pushed away from him. "Dammit. Tell me what I can do to make you change your mind and let Shelby and the baby stay."

"Do?" he asked thoughtfully after a minute. "Ante up, Kate. It's time to put in or fold. I want you."

"Me?" Her knees were wobbling now and she was becoming light-headed. "You mean to be your *maîtresse?*"

He chuckled at her use of the old-fashioned word. "A mistress? Now wouldn't *that* be an amusing form of revenge."

She scowled and clutched his arm. "You can't mean that. You don't even know who I am anymore."

Kate clearly understood that Chase was her biggest weakness. She *wanted* him to want her. But she would never give up independence—not even for him. If he asked for her body, fine. She would be all for it.

He would never take her soul.

"No?" Chase said with a chuckle. "Well, let's start with dinner, then. Tomorrow night. And wear something sexy. I think I'll be needing a lot of persuasion."

# Three

*Chase knelt beside Kate under the low-hanging branches of a willow tree that was all decked out in its June finest. Silvery light from the full moon shone through the leaves in platinum streaks and illuminated Kate's sweet, smiling face. Taking his time, he unbuttoned her blouse and ran a finger over the rise of her creamy breasts, peeking out from under the soft, white bra.*

*Kate, his wonderful darling. Tonight wouldn't be the first time that they'd made love, but this time he would go slow. He would manage to ignore the hard, burning heat in his groin long enough to make it good for her, too. Tonight he would show her…tell her with both his touch and his words how much a part of him she had become.*

*"I love you, Kate," he whispered as he bent to place a kiss against her tender neck. "You are my everything."*

*"Chase," she groaned. "That feels so good. But I have something important to tell you."*

*"Tell me, chère," he mumbled against her lips. "Tell me how you feel."*

*She opened her mouth to speak, and he held his breath, expecting to hear words of love for the very first time in his whole nineteen years of life.*

*"Whoohoo. Just looky what we've got here."*

*The sudden deep catcall from behind his back shot a spear of fear straight to his gut. But before he could cover Kate and turn around, rough hands grabbed them both and pulled them out from under their shelter.*

Chase shot up out of bed with a start. His hands were fisted, the sweat poured off his forehead and the sheets lay on the floor in a tangled knot.

Dammit. He hadn't had that dream in years.

Looking around the bedroom of his suite at the B&B, he tried to get his bearings—tried to remember how to breathe. He grabbed his slacks off the back of a chair, pulled them on and opened the French doors out to his private balcony.

In three long strides he was outside, holding on to the railing with a deadly grip. He stared unseeing out at the pearly gray predawn that was casting quiet shadows over the southern Louisiana swamp.

He took a deep breath and blew it out. It hadn't occurred to him that coming back here and facing his past would bring back that dream. He should've known.

In fact, he should welcome the old dream, though it always left his body aching for Kate and his soul starved for words that never came. The familiar dream scene was not the worst thing that had happened that fateful

June night so long ago. The pain of betrayal was much harder to live with. But the dream of Kate lying under him and looking up with what should've been love in her eyes was the memory that hurt the most.

That look had been all a lie. And he needed to keep the pain fresh in his mind when he dealt with Kate now.

A lone Snowy Egret caught his attention as it swooped low in the skies between the B&B and the swamp. It was a beautiful and graceful sight with its white plumes and its slow, gliding movements. But all the bird's solo flight succeeded in doing was driving home the point that Chase had lived with for most of his life.

He was a loner and had been happily content with his own company for as long as he could remember. A solitary man who needed no one and should expect nothing that he didn't make for himself.

Kate stopped walking and looked up, watching the Snowy Egret as it glided past and headed out toward the Gulf. It was exactly this kind of beautiful sight she would miss the most if she had to leave town and her home to find work in the city.

She lowered her head and trudged on down the ancient path, leading between Live Oak Hall and the mill. How many more times would she be allowed to make this trip in the quiet early hours? How many more times would she make the return trip, watching as the sunset streaked its fantastic rose and gold hues over her plantation home?

Everything depended on Chase now. Her father had never let her contribute ideas concerning her own destiny. Now it looked as if Chase was going to do the same thing.

When the outline of the mill came into view, she forced her slumping shoulders back into some semblance of a straight line. It had been a very long night, tossing and turning with the erotic flashes of Chase taking her into his arms and running his hands over her body.

She hadn't allowed herself to dream or even to think of those things in so many years it seemed like forever. But that whole scene with Chase on the B&B's terrace last night had stirred up more than just the dreams.

Taking her hands out of her jacket pockets, Kate looked down on her bandaged finger and thought about the sensual sensations that had rolled over her in waves as he sucked her finger into his mouth. It gave her chills even now as the sun was beginning to warm the landscape and the morning mists disappeared back into their hiding places in the dismal swamp.

If Chase was serious about making her his mistress in payment for letting Shelby stay in the guest house, she would happily jump right in. There wasn't much she could ever hope to do to repay him for the wrongs that had been done to him so long ago. The wrongs that she had helped create with her own stupid mistakes.

Seeing him make a success of the mill and living happily in Live Oak Hall wasn't anything she could have a real part in. Those were the kinds of things he would have to get for himself. Though he probably deserved to be given those things and much more from the town that had deserted him when he needed them the most.

But if he really still did want her…body, she would give it gladly. She knew herself well enough to know she would never let on to him that he could also have her heart—did have her heart—and always would. No, that would be giving him too much power. The two of them weren't meant for a future together, a fact she had accepted long ago with regret.

Kate stepped into the mill's office and removed her jacket. Listening for sounds that would tell her that Chase was already at work, the sound she heard instead was a soft crying sob. She followed it around a corner and found her secretary, sitting at her desk and bent over in tears.

"Rose? What's wrong?" Kate went to her and began patting her back.

"He's going to deliberately ruin us," Rose sobbed. "None of us will have a job. We'll all have to leave our homes."

"Shush, shush, *chère*. What makes you say these things? Is Chase here?"

Rose shook her head and looked up into Kate's eyes. "No, not yet. But the word is all over town. He's come for revenge and means to get even with everyone in Bayou City for how they treated him as a kid."

Kate leaned over to put an arm around her secretary's shoulders. "Nonsense, Rose. You've lived in this place all your life. I can't imagine you'd start believing the town gossip at this late date when I'm positive you know better than that."

Besides, Kate thought grimly, the only people left here that Chase had a real reason to hate were her father and herself. And her father was beyond his reach now.

"Chase is obviously a successful businessman, Rose. I don't believe he would deliberately throw money away just to even an old score. He's much smarter than that."

"Thanks for the vote of confidence, *chère*." The deep sound of Chase's voice came from the doorway.

Kate twisted around to see him leaning against the threshold with his arms folded across his chest, studying her. "Chase. I didn't hear you…"

"But I don't need your support," he interrupted.

She stood up and sighed silently to herself. No, he would never allow her to give him anything. She knew that, but it stung all the same.

He narrowed his eyes to scrutinize her, and the close survey began to make her feel all itchy, like she'd forgotten to wash.

Chase took a couple of steps into the room toward her. "In fact, judging from how you look, I won't need anything from you today." He turned to address Rose. "Do you think you can show me where the files are without dissolving into a weepy mess, young woman?"

Rose sniffed once and nodded without opening her mouth.

"Fine." He turned back and lowered his voice to a growl. "Go home, Kate. You look terrible. I'll expect you to appear rested and at your best for our appointment this evening."

"But, Chase…"

"Go home. There's nothing you can do for me—until tonight."

Kate fisted her hands at her side and bit her tongue to keep from saying something she would forever regret. Chase was acting like a real jerk, but she knew he was a different person deep inside. He just couldn't have changed that much in ten years. But he did have reason enough to hate her, and there was nothing she could ever do or say to fix things.

So she clamped her mouth shut and turned away,

running from the memories. Running from her heart. And running from the pain of accepting the consequences of her past.

Chase drove a hand through his hair and leaned back in the desk chair. He couldn't seem to concentrate on the damn accounts when all he could think of were the deep-purple smudges that had been under Kate's eyes and the bone-weary slouch of her shoulders this morning.

He'd come to Bayou City with the intention of hearing her beg…for the mill…for her home. And if the truth were known, to beg for his forgiveness.

But he hadn't liked hearing her beg for a friend and that friend's baby, or to see her looking so emotionally bruised. It didn't sit well with his memories.

He was trying to reconcile what he felt now with all the built-up hatred from ten years of believing her to be someone he despised. To see her looking melancholy and fragile this morning had ripped big holes in his plans…and in his soul.

It was midafternoon and it was time to accept the fact that he really did need Kate to interpret some of the mill's figures for him. He would have to give it up for today and begin again tomorrow when she could help.

He dismissed the secretary for the rest of the afternoon, put the convertible top down and climbed into his Jag. Intending to go straight back to the B&B to dress for dinner, he was surprised to find himself on the canal road and heading toward the shack where he had spent his youth.

Chase knew the house had stood empty for five years

now, ever since he'd spirited his father away in the middle of the night and delivered the old man to a rehab clinic in Houston to dry out.

But something inside him must've wanted to see the old place. He needed to refresh his harsh memories, and what better place than the run-down house he had always hated.

That shack had forever been the bane of his existence. The kids at school teased him unmercifully about his dirt-poor circumstances and about his father the drunk. The other kids' parents didn't want them to hang out with such trash. Everything that had ever gone wrong in town had been somehow connected to Chase or his father, "that drunk Severin."

Not that Chase had ever been in any real trouble. Just a few fights and a day or two suspension from school for those times when he'd not shown so he could sober up his father. But the word about him being bad to the bone got around anyway.

He had no family to fight for him. No brothers, cousins or uncles to cover his back like every other boy hereabouts in St. Mary Parish. So he learned early how to take care of himself—and how not to trust anyone.

Too bad his lessons hadn't extended to Kate. Despite the fact that her father was the most powerful man in town and always had it in for him and his father, Chase had let her get under his defenses. The pain of her betrayal still stung after all these years.

Driving along in the sun, he noticed that nothing much seemed to have improved in the town of his childhood. If anything, the whole place seemed a little shabbier than in his memories. The businesses in town gave way to two-story clapboard houses and finally to what could easily be called shanties as he drove down the gravel and mud road that ran alongside the no-name canal.

He slowed as he passed by the last decent house on the road and saw his former neighbor Irene Fortier sitting on her front porch. She waved at him and stood, so he brought the car to a stop beside the yard in order to speak to her.

If it hadn't been for Irene five years ago, Chase wouldn't have known that his father had been lying comatose in his bed for twenty-four hours. She'd found his dad and had called to ask for help.

Chase had come at once. Nothing, neither bad memories nor business commitments, would've stopped him from helping his father. But he didn't let anyone else in town know he was there, and he certainly hadn't stayed long.

"Hello, *cher,*" Irene said as he stepped out of the car. "I heard the rumors that you were back in town."

He nodded but eased away when she went to kiss his cheek. Her flower print dress and the homey smells of cooking lingered in his brain and reminded him of how much he'd always liked being around Irene as a kid.

"You've come home to move back in?"

"No, Irene. I'm not sure why I'm down on Canal Road this afternoon. Guess I just wanted to see how much damage the elements have done to Dad's shack."

"It's about the same as always. I've been seeing to keeping the critters and the bums out."

"Thanks." He wasn't sure he really thanked her for her efforts. Maybe he would've been happier to know the place had burned down and taken all the old hurts along with it.

"You plan on staying in Bayou City?" Irene asked.

"Only long enough to exorcise old ghosts."

Irene studied him from behind the plastic-rimmed eyeglasses she wore. "You own the mill now, I've heard. You here to get even with people, son?"

He'd thought that's why he had come home. But now... The memories of Irene's goodness, finding the town in such sad straits and the odd tenderness he'd felt when Kate had asked his help for a friend and not herself made him want to reconsider his intentions.

Hell. Not sure of his own motivations anymore, Chase ignored Irene's question and asked one of his own. "Did you ever meet my grandmother Steele? Did she ever come to Bayou City? I don't remember meeting her or even hearing her name when I was a kid."

Irene shook her head sadly. "No, child. Your mother, Francine, died believing her own mother hated her for marrying your father. I tried to encourage Francine to call Lucille when the time was getting close for your birth." Irene hesitated and sighed. "I think she might've done it eventually...if she'd lived."

Chase had no memory of his mother, only pictures and the stories that Irene had told him when he'd been little. He didn't have any reason to grieve for a woman that he'd never known. But inheriting money and a family from her had made him rather sorry that they'd missed talking to each other.

"Why did my mother marry my father, Irene?" Knowing what he'd learned recently about Lucille Steele and her family, he couldn't imagine now why a young woman from such a good home would run off and marry the town drunk.

Irene laughed. "Love would be my guess. But that's a question that you should ask of your father."

Chase remembered asking his father lots of family questions as a boy. Only he'd never gotten any answers. He'd learned early that simply asking the questions only made his father sink further into the drunken stupor that had been his old man's constant companion back then.

Today, his father wanted to talk, but Chase couldn't manage to listen. There was too much heartache in the past for him to forgive.

He shrugged off Irene's suggestion. "Someday maybe."

After he'd said goodbye to Irene, he spun the Jag around in her front yard and headed back to the B&B. There wasn't time now to go look at the old shack.

And that was really for the best. Too much thinking and talk about his childhood unsettled him, and he wanted to be sharp for his confrontation with Kate tonight.

Something had snapped in him when he'd seen her out on the terrace last night. His whole body ached to touch her—to taste her—once again.

His gut clenched and his mouth watered at the mere thought of her. Those weren't the reactions he thought he would have after all this time of hating her. But there it was. Nothing to do but make the most of it.

The best restaurant around was not in Bayou City but fifteen miles away at a country crossroads closer to New Iberia. A place where it was usually impossible to get a table at the last minute, the owner of Kizzy's Café greeted Chase like an old friend and seated them in a private corner at a booth set for two.

Everything was so lovely. Kate marveled at the eclectic feel of the antique country store that had been turned into a modern Cajun fine dining establishment. Crisp, white tablecloths, mismatched chairs and cozy booths hidden in secret corners. Heavy blue pottery dishes, and centerpieces of baby pink roses in shiny silver vases.

Her friend Shelby had first learned to cook as an employee of this restaurant before Madeleine was born. But Kate herself had never been in the place.

Looking around to see if she knew any of the other diners, Kate was pleased to see that no one else in the place had taken any notice of them. The gossip around town about her and Chase had already reached epic proportions. If anyone from Bayou City saw them out together it would only make things much worse.

The waiter brought a bottle of expensive sauvignon blanc at Chase's request and poured a small amount into a glass, offering to let Chase decide if it was to his taste.

But Chase shook his head. "Give the lady the choice." He turned to her as the waiter offered her the glass. "You're the aristocrat. You know much more about wine than I ever will, I'm sure."

Kate tried the wine and silently nodded at the waiter to pour and then leave the bottle. It looked as if Chase wasn't going to miss any opportunity to embarrass her tonight. Well, she could take it.

She would take much more than embarrassment from him. But what exactly was it that he wanted—or expected?

Who was this Chase Severin? What had he become in the ten years since he'd left town?

Chase rejected the menus when the waiter offered them. Instead he knew exactly what he wanted. He ordered crawfish pie, red beans and rice and jambalaya for both of them. They were all typical Cajun dishes, but she'd heard that Kizzy's served the very best in the world.

It made her wonder if the place's fame had reached Chase's ears in…wherever he'd been living.

"Uh…" she began hesitantly. "You know where I've been and what I've been doing for the last ten years. But I was wondering…"

"If the rumors were true?" he cut in. "If I had earned my fortune by gambling?"

"No…I mean…sort of. I was just curious to know what you've been doing all this time."

He leaned back in the booth, stretched his legs and crossed his ankles under the table. The candlelight made it difficult to see his expression clearly. But she could feel the heat of his gaze—right through her clothes.

"I am a gambler, Kate. I'd say most of my life has been spent in one gamble or another."

He let that thought hang in the air for a few moments. Did he mean that he'd taken a gamble on her years ago? A gamble that he felt he'd lost? She sensed the pink sting of a blush crawling up her neck.

"After I left…or was escorted out of…Bayou City," he began again, "I hitched a ride to New Orleans. Found my way into a backroom poker game or two until I had enough for a real stake. Then I made my way to Las Vegas."

He stopped and took a sip of water, ignoring his

wine. "I turned pro, hit a couple of major pots and eventually won a casino in a high-stakes private game."

"A whole casino? Wow."

He chuckled. "Yeah, it was pretty wow for a twenty-one-year-old kid. I quit playing and decided to limit all my gambling to the business end of the casino."

"You must've done fairly well with it," she murmured as she took a sip from her wineglass.

"You could say that. After a couple of years, I doubled down and bought another house, then a few more in Reno and Atlantic City."

"So that's what you do now? You own casinos all over the country?" He was rich enough to make Kate nervous.

"Casinos, hotels, resorts, restaurants. A few of them I acquired in payment of bad debts. Most I bought for pennies on the dollar and turned them around."

"Well, it'll cost you a pretty penny to put the mill to rights, if that's your newest gamble."

"I've *got* a pretty penny, *chère*. In fact, I've just inherited enough pennies to make your beautiful head swim."

"Inherited? Not from your father. He hasn't died?"

Chase shook his head. "No, not my father. It turns out that I have a whole respected family on my mother's side. My grandmother died recently, and I was one of the main beneficiaries to her rather vast fortune."

"Oh, *cher*," she said, genuinely happy for him. "I didn't know you had any family except for your father."

"Neither did I. Funny how things in life can turn around so suddenly, isn't it?"

Was that another none-too-subtle hint about her new dire circumstances? It didn't matter. She was glad he had found wealth, relatives and respect. Regardless of the fact that it meant he had control of her future now.

Chase had always been the one really good guy in town in her mind. The good guy who had protected her and towered over everyone else in her estimation.

She'd never doubted that he would do his best for the town. And soon the rest of the world would know it, too.

The waiter brought their salads, then their entrees, and the time passed quietly while they enjoyed their meals. After the chicory coffee was served and the candles on the table had burned low, Chase tried to clear his head of the congenial feelings and the sensual images that had been plaguing him during their dinner.

Kate was too bright—too soft—too everything. In her sleeveless black dress with the little shoulder straps and the dainty high-heel sandals, the woman made his insides ache with wanting.

He'd meant for this to be a fast meal where he could study her, find ways to get under her skin and make her want him. Instead, he'd opened his mouth and his heart and told her things about his past that few people had ever heard.

Dumb. Well, he would just have to begin again. After all, his original intentions were to have her squirm, right?

"You ready to leave yet, Kate?"

"Leave? Where are we going? Is the evening over already? I wanted to explain to you…"

"Nothing's over. Get your things together. I'll take care of the bill and then we're going home."

"Home? To the B&B?"

He stood back, studying her and waiting for the reaction. "To *my* home, *chère*. We're going to Live Oak Hall. I have a game I think you might enjoy playing."

He waited for the question. But though her eyes were wide, she raised her chin and didn't say a word. The ache in his chest from wanting her and yet trying to remember that he hated her was beginning to make him irritable. Why couldn't this be easy? Why couldn't she just be the heartless witch of his nightmares?

"I'm going to give you the chance to gamble for what you want," he muttered. "You want something from me, you have to win it."

"I'm not much of a gambler," Kate told him quietly.

"Ah, but this game will be so enjoyable." He slid out of the booth and turned back, holding out his hand to her.

Finally she asked, "What game is that?" Ignoring his hand, she scooted out of the booth on her own.

"Let's just see how badly you want your favor." He took her arm and leaned in to whisper in her ear. "A little game of poker ought to tell us all we need to know. Don't you agree, *bébé?*"

"Which poker? I'm not good at playing card games."

"It's better if you're bad at it, Kate. This is the very best game to play between two old friends, and one I know *I'll* enjoy—strip poker."

# Four

"That's cheating, Kate." Chase said the words with a low growl, but his eyes were dark with mischief and mirth.

"A shoe is an article of clothing," she insisted.

After already removing her watch, a ring and the clip from her hair, shoes were the only things left to go before the consequences of being a loser in this game became much too intimate.

"Besides, I think you're the one that's cheating," Kate argued. "The cards you've been dealing are just awful."

Chuckling softly, Chase shook his head. "I don't have to cheat. You're terrible at this game." He leaned back and leered at her through the flickering candlelight. "But the article of clothing is a *pair* of shoes. You can't lose only one of the pair."

"Hmm. All right." Kate grudgingly removed both shoes.

Trying to slow down the inevitable, she took a long, deep sip of brandy. Her hand was trembling, but she wasn't afraid. Kate just didn't want Chase to know how badly he was getting to her. After years of dreaming about his touch and his kiss, she desperately wanted to lose this game. But she didn't want him to know his advantage. Her blood and her brain were sizzling by simply being this close to him.

They were sitting on the oriental rug at the foot of the massive hearth in the formal parlor of her ancestral home. Chase lit the fire to dispel the chill, and had insisted on candlelight and after-dinner drinks for their poker game.

She lowered her eyes and took one more sip, letting the warmth of the smooth liquid roll down her throat. But when she finally looked up, he was watching her with a wicked gleam and a shadowed expression. Cruel secrets entwined about them like a swamp full of tangled kudzu.

Chase dealt another hand. The cards lay facedown at her place. She could hear them silently call her name, taunting her to turn them up and learn her fate.

"Your action, Kate."

Finally she forced herself to pick up her hand. She knew in an instant it was a winner—a full house, jacks high.

"Wha…" She cleared her throat and reminded herself to keep a poker face. "What stakes did you have in mind this time, Chase? There's nothing much left for me to wager except the dress and my underwear."

"The dress will do," he said with a lazy drawl.

"Fine. But if I win I want your promise to consider letting Shelby and the baby stay in the guest cottage."

"You're not much on bluffing, *chère*. Have a good hand, do you? Remind me to teach you someday how to keep a straight face over a decent hand.

"But for now," he added with a slow grin. "Let's see what you've got. I'll call."

It was time to lay out her cards. She quietly fanned them open before her, trying hard not to gloat.

Until…Chase soberly turned over his cards and Kate felt her stomach jump and begin doing backflips.

"Four kings?" she groaned in amazement. Stunned by his outrageous good fortune, Kate sat there immobile and stared at the cards.

Reality hit her all too suddenly when she felt Chase reach over to lightly finger one of her dress's straps. Shocked by the warm, erotic sensation of his hands on her bare skin, Kate gasped and drew away. Then she cursed herself as an idiot. Draw away? When this was what she wanted, after all?

"I won that dress fair and square," Chase said in a ragged whisper. "But I would never force you to do anything you didn't want to do. You can trust me not to hurt you."

"Oh, Chase," she mumbled past an unexpected lump in her throat. "Those are the very first words you ever said to me. Do you remember?"

She glanced over at him just as a drape of moonlight fell across his face, revealing hard features and a tense jawline. "That was in another lifetime, Kate. Things have changed."

Not for her they hadn't. "I remember being ten years old like it was yesterday." The memory burned into her soul. "My mother had just…run away… And when we discovered she'd meant to go for good, my father simply shrugged and said 'good riddance to bad trash.' I never forgave him for that…never."

"You were a pretty tough cookie back then," Chase agreed. "You got it into your head to leave town, too."

Chase's voice began to mellow as he moved back into the shadows out of her sight. "I remember the scrawny dark-haired kid with the chip on her shoulder who wandered way out to the wrong side of town and then got lost. You were all full of fight and ready to conquer the world."

"I wasn't lost," she said with a smile of memory. "Just spitting mad. But you and your father wiped my nose, filled my stomach and gently convinced me to go on back home. It was one of the kindest things anyone ever did for me." And she had fallen desperately, madly, irrevocably in love with Chase from that first moment.

"Did your mother ever contact you again? Do you know where she is now?" The husky voice coming out of the darkness carried a note of concern. "You could hire private detectives to look for her. That's how my grandmother Steele's lawyers found me."

"No. It doesn't matter anymore." Her heart twinged as she realized he truly cared about her welfare even after everything that had happened in the past.

But then the sound of his voice turned cold. "You quit fighting years ago, didn't you?" he asked with a sneer.

She knew he was referring to that last night. That last horrible night when her whole world had collapsed. But she didn't want to talk about it. Not now.

This was no night for recriminations and revelations.

Tonight she wanted to feel his hands on her body, his tongue tasting, stirring—at long, long last.

"My mother's whereabouts don't matter," she told him as she raised her chin. "If she wanted me—wanted to see me—she would've done it by now. I've grown up and don't need a mother anymore."

A tense moment of silence worried Kate and made her notice a drop of sweat that had formed at her temple. What was he thinking?

"Is that what you imagined of me all this time, Kate? That if I'd wanted to see you, I would've contacted you? It didn't occur to you to try to find me first?"

She shook her head sadly. "I was positive that you wouldn't want to see me…that you hated me. I…I don't blame you for it, but I couldn't…" Her words trailed off and she let her chin drop again as she battled the tears.

This wasn't what she wanted to happen this evening. Couldn't they just take comfort from each other and forget the past for one night?

"I didn't…I don't…hate you, *chère*." For the moment Chase's voice was filled with painful emotion.

Wanting badly to put the past behind them forever, Kate almost blurted out the truth of what had really happened that last night. Then she thought better of it as she realized such a confession would mean the end of her time with him. If Chase didn't hate her now, he surely would when he heard it all. And she was becoming desperate for a few more hours…a few more days…with the only man she would ever love.

So because she loved him, because she couldn't bear to hear this strong man's indecision on her account, and because she would never welsh on a bet, Kate decided to pay up.

Slowly she got to her feet and pushed the spaghetti straps down her shoulders. Reaching behind her, she began to lower the back zipper, but found that her hands were shaking too violently to get the job done.

Suddenly clumsy, Kate felt the sting of embarrassment rising up her chest and flaming her cheeks. She had on the sexiest underwear she owned—in black lace—as she had expected and hoped—that Chase would undress her sometime tonight. He'd said he wanted her as a mistress, hadn't he?

But she'd never expected to have to do a striptease for the man. It made her feel naughty…scandalous. And that was so far from her ordinary existence that she was left floundering and brainless.

She heard something rustling in the dark shadows surrounding her and felt a whisper of air against her skin.

"Need help, *chère?*" Chase's rough, masculine voice came from close behind her instead of from the other direction, raising the hair on her arms and sending a chill down her spine.

Kate wanted to spin around and face him. Seeing Chase's eyes as she took off the dress became suddenly terribly important. But his strong hands took her by the shoulders and kept her facing the other way.

"Stay still," he ordered softly. "I'll take care of the zipper. But you need to hold your hair out of the way."

He took his hands off her shoulders but remained close enough that his breath blew warmth across her chilled skin. How could she be both cold and too hot at the same time?

Wishing this part of the evening would hurry up and be over so Chase would finally take her to bed, Kate did as he requested. With jerky movements, she managed to lift her hair and hold it off her neck.

"Sweet," he murmured in her ear. His voice ran along her nerve endings, stirring her senses and arousing her desire.

The soft music of the zipper being lowered sounded for all the world like summer insects buzzing far off in the deep swamp. She felt light-headed and achy as the satin material of the black dress whispered against her skin, slid past her hips and pooled on the floor.

She stood perfectly still, naked save for her strapless bra and bikini panties, and prayed for Chase to touch her. His breathing was loud enough and ragged enough from behind her to let her know he was there and watching her. She felt his gaze, roaming over her, making the heat spike through her body.

Her own breathing became labored and shallow, echoing in her ears, while the sensation of being touched with just his eyes made her wet and ready for him. But he did not put his hands on her again.

She eased around, ready to make the first move toward kissing him if necessary. But Chase was not behind her. Only twitching shadows of firelight filled the space with empty echoes.

"Chase?"

"Game's over." His raspy voice came from the darkened doorway at the other side of the room. "You won. Shelby and the baby can stay."

"But, Chase…" She turned to see his silhouette.

"There's room enough in this old plantation house for everyone. I'll be moving in tomorrow."

"Into my bedroom?" She held her breath, waiting for an answer.

"We'll see," he said roughly. "I may not wish to sleep with old ghosts."

"What about tonight, Chase?"

"Go to bed. I've grown tired of the game. Good evening, Kate."

Through the low light dancing from the candles and fireplace, she watched as he turned his back and left the room. Choking back a sob, Kate sank to the floor and wrapped her arms around her waist.

He hadn't been turned on by her as she had been for him. Oh, Lord. Living in the same house but not sleeping with him was going to be a much worse punishment than being thrown out of her own home would've been. He couldn't have found a more perfect way to take revenge.

And the thing was…nothing that he'd done or could ever do would make her love die. She was doomed to a lifetime of misery, wishing for things to be different.

Chase eased onto a bar stool at the smoky roadhouse tavern, leaned his elbows on the broad mahogany bar and ordered a bottle of bourbon. It was almost closing time, but he figured the bottle could easily go with him when they kicked him out. He imagined they would have to call a cab for him—because he fully intended to get rip-roaring drunk before they closed the doors.

Squeezing his eyes shut, he tried to close his mind to the picture of Kate standing there in front of the fireplace in nothing but two pieces of black lace. Her scent was still in his nostrils. The heat from her back still burned his knuckles.

He wasn't sure he would be able to stick with his plan and stay here in Bayou City while he made a decision on the mill. Every time he looked at Kate he wanted to taste her.

Even from the distance of ten years he remembered the flavor of the tender skin at the back of her neck. Remembered the spun honey of her dusky nipples, puckering under the ministrations of his tongue. And tasted in his mind the sweetness of the silky flesh covering the pulse beat right above her breasts.

Oh, God. He poured himself a shot and slugged it back. The fiery liquid burned all the way down as he perversely savored the pain roaring in his gut. He deserved to ignite in hell.

He couldn't get her out of his mind. So many nights since he'd last seen her ten years ago had been spent dreaming of those dark eyes, sparkling in the glow of moonlight as she reached out for him.

Now he would never be rid of the picture of her standing there before him tonight, half-naked, shivering and hanging her head as she removed her dress. Even in the flickering light, he had clearly seen her distress. And he damned himself for it.

Pushing her too far had been his objective. Making her squirm the way he had years ago had been the goal. But he hadn't counted on seeing the grown-up Kate, looking so erotic and earthy and so made for sex— flaming under the blush of embarrassment.

It had thrown him. Made him think.

He'd ached for the pleasure of her body. Her long

legs had seemed to go on forever, her porcelain skin just begged to be stroked. But he would not take her…or anyone, against their free will.

Swearing under his breath, Chase tried to examine the emotion that had overcome his desire for revenge and that had even managed to push aside his lusty urges. The emotion that had shocked him…driving him right out of the house and into this bar.

Need. Pure gut-wrenching need—to protect her. To hold her and keep her safe in a dangerous world.

What a fool he'd been to think he could tease Kate, bring her to desperation and then casually take her. There had never been anything casual about the way he felt about Kate. And now he knew there never would be.

Chase reached for the bottle, poured another shot and downed the bourbon without ever tasting a thing past his own desolation.

"Trying to outdrink your old man, Severin?"

Looking up and focusing on the ancient bartender for the first time, Chase plastered a furious scowl across his face and narrowed his eyes. "Robert Guidry? I thought you'd be dead and buried by now. Leave me alone."

"Yeah," the old Cajun chuckled. "That'd be just exactly what Charles Severin would've said. How y'all are?"

"Go away."

The bartender studied him for a moment. "You got the look, boy. Sure enough. Lost love, same as Charles. It's bad medicine, you coming back here just to become a drunk."

"That's not why I'm here," Chase mumbled. But something the old bartender said got him to thinking. "You knew my father when he was young, didn't you?"

The bartender swiped a cloth across the sleek wood and nodded. "All of us raised up in the same parish. You included."

"Did my father always drink too much? What was he like when he went to school? Was he a hell-raiser?"

"Charles Severin was smart as a whip, he was," the older man said through a half smile. "His mother was widowed young and Charles became the man of the family as a boy. Never knew him to touch a drop of the liquid madness. He worked. Went to school. Most everybody liked him."

"Then what happened? Why did he start drinking?"

Shaking his head sadly, the bartender lowered his voice to a rasp. "I remember the day Charles came home from college, toting along his pretty young wife. Never saw any man so crazy in love. He worshiped that woman. They planned on building a good life here in Bayou City."

"So what changed?"

"Your momma died. She wasn't strong enough for childbirth like the other women round here. From that day forward...well...Charles, he just couldn't seem to face the days—or the nights without her."

Of course that was it, Chase thought. His father had loved his mother. And then when she'd died, he'd ended up wishing the child they'd created had died in her place.

It hurt, but it made sense. His father had never been a cruel man, but sometimes it'd felt like he couldn't bear to look at his only son without a few drinks under his belt.

Chase reached for the bottle again, but stilled his hand before he could pour the shot. Drinking had never solved his father's problems in all those years and it wasn't likely to do much for Chase's now, either.

Dammit.

He stood up and pulled a few bills from his pocket. "Thanks for the history lesson, Guidry. I'll be going now."

"Oh, I got lots more lessons to tell, boy. You stick around and I'll be glad to learn you."

Shaking his head, Chase grinned at the old man. "Not tonight, thanks. Maybe some other time." He threw the money on the bar and turned to leave.

The old bartender waylaid him with a hand on his arm. "You in trouble, son? You've got the witching about you. I see it plain as day."

"The witching?" A sudden chill ran up Chase's spine. But he cursed himself as an idiot for letting his imagination go. "What are you talking about?"

"The magic," Guidry hissed. "The minute you touched your pocket, a golden mist came down over you. Some witch is stirring with your soul, boy. Better watch out."

Nonsense. But Chase's first reflex was to reach into his pocket for the gypsy's gift. He palmed the jewel-covered egg. There was nothing unusual about the warm metallic feel of the gold.

See there. The old Cajun was just letting his superstitions run away with him. Chase had lived in these parts long enough to know that magic couldn't touch you unless you believed. And he didn't.

He bade the bartender a good night and headed back toward the B&B. It had been one hell of a day, and moving into Live Oak Hall tomorrow was going to take every last bit of his attention and resolve.

Gritting his teeth, Chase fisted his hands and swallowed the sickening feeling that he had just stepped into shifting sands that would pull him in far over his head. "What in hell have I gotten myself into?"

The old gypsy woman pushed back from the table and spit out a curse. "So you don't believe in the magic, young Severin? How foolhardy."

Passionata waved a hand over the crystal and crossed her arms over her chest. She had a good mind to let him stew forever with his own ghosts.

The minute she'd thought it, however, the gypsy king's voice, bidding her to keep his deathbed legacy, came back to haunt her. If she didn't spend the extra time on Chase Severin's inheritance, her father would never rest—would never let her rest.

"Bah!" She had a feeling that delivering this magic to such a nonbeliever might just be the death of her.

Wearily she rose up and sighed. There was nothing to do but to go there.

She slid the crystal into a deep pocket and prepared to face the stifling musk of the hidden marshes once again. The stealthy swamp was her old friend. She would make her way back to the jungles, black waters and mosquitoes.

Moonlight and cypress knees awaited her arrival with promise. Young Severin had met his match.

"I am what you have gotten into, boy," she whispered to him on the winds. "And I am prepared to be the winner of this game."

# Five

Chase drove his Jag down the sun-dappled road that skirted Blackwater Bayou on his way to Live Oak Hall. When the car came out from under the clouds of tree branches with their dripping Spanish moss, he found himself roaring down the blacktop that ran parallel to the mill.

He grimaced at his first clear view of that monstrous ghost. The old rice mill was a pure eyesore. He slowed the car and pulled off on the shoulder to study it a little better from this distance.

He remembered thinking as a kid that the mill resembled a giant beehive, always busy with activity and noisy with people making a living. It was the center of commerce for the whole town, sometimes for the whole parish.

In his memory he saw lines of trucks hauling in raw

rice twenty-four hours a day, and seagoing barges leaving from the deep-water port to take the milled rice all over the world. But today, on a sunny Saturday morning, it looked deserted and forlorn.

The people of this town and the surrounding countryside once had employment and prosperity—way back when Kate's grandfather ran things. But the old man had died when Chase was a teen and Kate's father had taken over. Now, thanks to years of mismanagement, the citizens had nothing but layoffs and a huge rusting derelict of a building.

Chase had originally come home ready to destroy the mill, thinking that because it had once been run by Kate's despicable father and represented his incompetent power, it deserved to go up in smoke. But Henry Beltrane was dead and buried. And Chase's anger at the town for turning their backs on him when he needed them the most seemed like an ancient bad dream.

The childhood hometown he had hated and loved was now twisting in the wind, left to rot away all by itself. And the thought of that gave him absolutely no pleasure. It only made him sad.

His attitude toward Kate was much more conflicted. Sometimes when Chase looked at her, ice water ran through his veins, freezing his heart to her predicament. At other times, just one glimpse flamed his blood and burned a path right through his hardened soul.

Somehow when she was near, old half-remembered dreams assailed him with soft sighs and warm waves of staggering desires. He didn't know what to do about the weakness she brought to him. But destroying a whole town just to hear her beg would make him every bit as contemptible as old Henry Beltrane had ever been.

Chase shook off both the anger and the desire. There were no easy solutions here.

Looking back at the rotting hulk of the mill, he still had to wonder if it was worth trying to save. Or if he had the expertise to even try. He was a well-known turnaround magician when it came to bringing casinos and resorts back to life. But he wasn't sure at all that he could be a miracle worker for a dying rice mill.

Slowly Chase pulled the Jag back onto the blacktop road and headed toward Live Oak Hall. For today he would not think of the mill. He would not consider his narrow choices on that account.

For today he would take the step that had always seemed so unimaginable when he'd been the boy from the wrong side of town. Today was the day when he would move into Live Oak Hall and make his mark as the richest man in town.

Deep down, somewhere in the very dark recesses of his mind, Chase knew that just the change of address would not really give him the social standing and admiration he so craved. But he brushed the knowledge aside along with the rest of the cobwebs in his dusty memory. Today was his day. There could be no room for second guesses or self-examinations.

A few minutes later he guided the Jag down the oak allée toward the portico of the plantation. With a deep breath of early-spring air, Chase pulled up at the front door and climbed out of the car.

*He was home.*

Dragging his luggage from the narrow backseat, Chase let his mind go blank, allowing himself to just feel. Being here felt right. Though, he remembered a time when he would have been arrested for trespassing if Kate's father had caught him anywhere on the property. Getting to see Kate back then had been tricky, full of secrets and sneaking around behind her father's back.

Chase shook out the remnants of memories and walked toward the house. The veranda was bathed in comforting shade as he moved up the front steps. Sun had warmed the air, birds chirped, bees stayed busy at the flowers.

But when he set his bags down to knock at the front door, Chase noticed some of the floorboards were hanging loose from their joints and bits of paint had begun to peel off of decades-old exterior walls. He looked closer and found cobwebs lurking in dark, dingy corners of the veranda.

Apparently the maintenance had been ignored for quite some time. A flash of anger at Kate for letting things slide came—and quickly went. This much deterioration had to have begun with her father. Princess Kate would know no better. No sense blaming her for things she hadn't done. There were plenty of other things for which she deserved the blame.

"Welcome, Chase." The alto voice was feminine but not Kate's.

He turned to see a slight woman in her midtwenties with ash-blond hair and soft-gray eyes, standing at the open door with a toddler in her arms. It was the quiet look in the woman's eyes that made the schoolday memories reel forward in his mind.

"Hello, Shelby," he murmured. "It's been a while."

She stood aside and let him move through the doorway. "Ten years. This is my daughter, Madeleine. We've been expecting you this morning."

"How do you do, Madeleine," Chase said to the serious baby with the big blue eyes, before he returned his attention to her mother. "Kate tells me you and your daughter are living in one of the guest cottages, Shelby. You divorced?"

Shelby chuckled, turned and headed toward the sweeping, main staircase. "You get right to the basics, don't you, Severin? No, I am not divorced. Maddie's father was a marine. Went off and got himself killed before he even knew he had a child on the way. And no, I'm not his widow, either. We weren't married."

Chase followed Shelby up the wide, carpeted stairs. He could easily see now why Kate had wanted to help this woman and her child. Her story had disturbed him a great deal, and he barely knew her.

"Kate didn't mention which room you'd be wanting to occupy," Shelby said when she reached the top of the staircase. "I try to keep up with the cleaning, but I didn't know you were moving in until this morning. If you want one of the rooms that isn't made up, it'll only take me twenty minutes or so to…"

"Would you mind giving me a short tour of the house first?" He still did not know what his own intentions were. "Where's Kate?"

Shelby moved the baby to her hip and gestured to the faded carpet. "Leave your luggage here on the landing. I'll show you around. Kate is outside doing Saturday chores."

"Kate? Doing chores? You're kidding."

"Hold it, Severin," Shelby said as she stopped and poked a finger at his chest. "You've been gone a long time. Maybe before you just jump to conclusions, you might want to take the time to really see the way things are now."

He dropped his luggage and smiled at the irate woman and her child. "Point taken." Chase wasn't sure he would be able to stand spending enough time here to see anything though, not with all the unwanted feelings that kept getting dredged up whenever he was around Kate. "Lead on with the tour."

For the next half hour Shelby showed him through the ten upstairs bedrooms, the kitchen, dining room, library and four parlors. Everything was clean but shabby. It made him melancholy to think of a grand historical house like this one falling into such disrepair.

Finally they arrived back at the base of the main staircase. "You won't need to make up a room for me," he said before they could climb the front stairs again. "I'll store my luggage for today and Kate and I will work out the sleeping arrangements later. Thanks."

Shelby released the baby on the marble floor, letting her crawl free. "No problem. Do you mind if I ask you a personal question? Something's been bothering me for ages."

He figured the way she'd hesitated that she wasn't curious about his plans for either the house or the mill. Good thing. Because Chase had no clue as to what he had in his own mind to do about them.

"Ask whatever you want," he said with a chuckle. "I reserve the right not to give you an answer."

She nodded thoughtfully. "Will you tell me what really happened that night ten years ago when you left town? I've heard tons of gossip about it over the years, but I'd like to know the true story."

"You haven't gotten the real story from Kate?"

Shelby folded her arms over her chest. "She won't talk about it. I was gone for the whole summer and part of that fall. By the time I came back, Kate…well…Kate was a different person from when I left."

"Different how?"

Shelby shrugged a shoulder. "I dunno. More serious, maybe. Certainly less fun loving and less popular with the other kids. She had stopped going to parties and worked much harder at getting good grades."

That didn't sound like the young Princess Kate he had left behind. But it did sound a little like the ice-princess rumors he'd heard since he'd been home.

"What about boyfriends? Dates?" he inquired.

"Not so much. In fact, none at all that last year in high school. But there have been a few guys since then. One, the good-looking tractor distributor from New Iberia, was real serious about Kate for a while. But she…she just never got into him.

"Then the word went around that Kate was, uh, frigid," Shelby continued hesitantly. "I actually think Kate believes that one herself."

Chase didn't buy it for a minute. He remembered the sizzle the two of them had created ten years ago. Kate had been the furthest thing from frigid then. And he'd seen the heat still there in her eyes just last night.

No. Kate was definitely not a cold fish. Not then. Certainly not now.

Shelby scooted over to her baby daughter and made sure the little girl hadn't put anything into her mouth, then she turned back to Chase. "So what happened to make you leave and to make Kate change so much?"

Chase wasn't sure talking about that night would be a good thing. But he hadn't ever told his side of the nightmare. Maybe it was past time.

"I have no idea what could have changed Kate," he said quietly. "But then, I left without knowing much of anything. I left in a hurry, before I could be run out of town bodily or locked up in the parish jail for good."

"Why?"

He shook his head. "Recently I've managed to piece together some of the puzzle about that night. But at the time, I was just as confused about why as anyone." He patted the breast pocket of his chambray shirt before he remembered that he'd quit smoking.

"It was the night of the prom," he began. "But Kate and I didn't go. We had a favorite place down by the river where we liked to…be together. We'd dream of the future and talk about what we wanted to do with our lives."

The years melted away in his mind, and through the mists of time he saw the young couple he and Kate had been—so desperately in love. With a start he amended that thought. *One* of them had been in love. The other was apparently a good liar.

He came back to the present with a thud. "Out of nowhere, four of the rougher guys we went to school with showed up and picked a fight for no reason. They weren't enemies of ours, but they were drunk and wouldn't talk—just started swinging.

"At first, I wasn't too concerned about taking them all on, they were pretty drunk…but then one of them grabbed Kate and ripped her shirt off. I guess I lost it. The next thing I knew the sheriff showed up and stopped me from killing the guy."

"You whipped all four boys?"

He tipped his chin. "They were drunk." It was still not something he was terribly proud of. "The one that had grabbed Kate ended up having to be taken to the hospital, and the sheriff said it was touch-and-go with him for a while."

"But why would the sheriff put you in jail?" Shelby asked. "They attacked you and Kate first."

"The other three boys gave a statement to the sheriff saying they'd seen me attacking Kate. They claimed they had been the ones to come to her rescue."

"What? Everyone in town knew you and Kate were a couple. Why would anyone believe such a thing?"

Chase drove his hand through his hair, wishing that he'd never started this trip down memory lane. Shelby was not going to like hearing what he had to say next.

"Kate told the sheriff it was true," Chase said in a low but clear voice. "She swore I'd been drinking and had dragged her out of the car and was attacking her when those boys came along and tried to save her."

Shelby's mouth dropped open, and for a minute she just stared at him. "I can't believe that."

Chase shook his head and gave her a wry smile. "I had some trouble with the concept at the time, too, but her old man turned up right then and offered me a deal. Henry Beltrane told me that because my father's family had been in the area for generations he would give me a break. If I'd leave town for good, he would see to it that no one pressed charges against me. I'd be in the clear, but I could never come home."

Shelby was still shaking her head. "There's something wrong with that story. I don't buy the part about Kate."

"It took me a few years to accept it myself. About six weeks ago I finally located the grown man that once was the boy I had put in the hospital. I never could understand why those kids were out there by the river that night. Nobody but Kate and I ever went to that place.

"Anyway, I found him working as a night security guard in New Orleans," Chase continued. "He confessed that Henry Beltrane had paid those four boys to find us and to beat me up…run me out of town. The rest of the story is that their fathers had been recently laid off from the mill and their families needed the money bad. But still…they had to get stone drunk to have the nerve to do such a thing."

"But why?" Shelby cried. "And why would Kate…?"

Chase shrugged. "Since that bastard Beltrane is dead, we'll never know his reasons."

Shelby looked so horrified that Chase decided to say something more. "I suspect that Kate must feel some guilt for her part since she refuses to talk to you about it."

"That story is just so unlike Kate," Shelby insisted. "I can't understand it."

All of a sudden, Chase knew he had said too much. "I can't understand it, either," he hedged. "But I didn't mean for these old ghost stories to come between the two of you."

"Oh, they won't," Shelby quickly told him. "That story has nothing to do with the Kate I know. And the Kate that I know saved my life."

Shelby reached over and swung her daughter up in her arms. The baby giggled before she nestled down against her mother's breast. "Right after Maddie was born…I thought I was going to have to give her up. I had nothing. No job and no family. I didn't have anywhere to live that would accept a baby, and I'd been begging friends for scraps of food.

"Kate's father was still alive at the time but he was sick," Shelby continued. "So Kate snuck us food and helped me fix up that old guest cottage out back so we'd have a place to stay. She even babysat so I could go round up some catering jobs."

Shelby placed a soft kiss against her child's forehead. "If I'd had to give up Maddie so soon after losing her daddy… Well, I wouldn't have wanted to go on. That's a fact. I owe Kate everything."

Chase was speechless. The two stories of Kate didn't mesh.

"I'm not going to ask Kate again what happened ten years ago," Shelby declared with a frown. "Eventually the truth will come out. It always does."

Chase nodded. He wasn't so sure he wanted to hear the whole truth himself. Sometimes secrets were best left buried.

The air in the house turned sticky—too close, stifling warm and still. He needed a fresh breath. Some way to clear his head.

He thanked Shelby for the welcome tour and stepped out the front door, looking for a little peace.

* * *

Kate hopped down off the rickety riding mower and dislodged the weeds that had glued themselves to the blades. She took a moment to put a hand on her lower back and stretch. It was a wicked, hot day for so early in the spring, and she could feel the sweat trickling down between her breasts.

Wiping a hand across her brow and glancing over to the house in the distance, Kate's vision cleared just in time for her to spot a movement on the front veranda. Confused, she looked around a little more and noticed Chase's car, parked in the shade of the front portico.

He was already here. Narrowing her eyes, she searched the shadows to find him. It was a little early yet, but it would be nice to get things settled between them.

She found him there all right, pacing up and down the long veranda. Tall and still so spectacularly good-looking women must fall madly in love with him at first glance, the sight of Chase this morning made her weak in the knees.

Looking cool and casual, he walked up and down past the double-wide front doors. He was wearing tight jeans and a chambray work shirt with the sleeves rolled up.

The image dragged out a ten-year-old memory that Kate had tried to lock away. It was of another too-hot spring day when the two of them had nothing in the world to worry about except where to find enough shade to have their picnic lunch.

She'd been sweaty on that day, too. But most of the heat in those days had come from their close, hard young bodies, holding on to each other as they frantically looked for a place to be together and to be alone with their desperate need.

Under a favorite willow, they had found shade and privacy. She remembered his touch…the way he tasted as his mouth crushed down on hers.

The faded memories by themselves were enough to perk up her breasts and send fire skittering down her spine. Kate blinked and tried to fight it, but a long-ago picture came to mind of Chase sitting beside her and watching her undress. He had imprisoned her and made her squirm by simply watching—and wanting—with those sinfully darkened eyes and fierce gaze.

The startling memory of him watching her undress opened her own eyes. No wonder last night's striptease had caused such erotic sensations in her body.

His heat had already scorched her as a girl. Blazed a sensual path down her body and tattooed her soul forever with his marker.

Back then, even as an inexperienced girl, Kate had climaxed just by staring into those dangerous steel-gray eyes. And she had fallen completely under the spell he had woven around them with soft words and tender touches.

As the sweat from the current steamy day rolled down her temples and blurred her vision, Kate swallowed past her dry throat and took a deep breath. She also remembered much too clearly the shy, coward of a girl she had been all those years ago. Too timid to seek out what she really wanted. Too eager to let the threat of scandal rule her desires and her life.

And much too afraid of her father's influence to go for her dreams.

But no more. Her father was dead. Everything she loved was on the verge of being lost forever. She could no longer afford to be a coward. Kate intended to ask for what she wanted from now on.

Chase fisted his hands on his hips and surveyed his property from the vantage point of the veranda. Though the landscape was scruffy and unkempt, the long vistas of grass and trees, spreading out for acres, gave him a world of satisfaction.

It was his…this land for as far as eyes could see… owning this land and coming from the right side of town had been his childhood dream. It made him briefly think about the old gypsy and her legacy gift—the gift that was supposed to bring him to his heart's desire.

The idea made him smile as he reached once more for the jeweled egg in his shirt pocket. Live Oak Hall had been his dream for as long as he could remember.

That old weird gypsy had been right. He had gotten his heart's desire.

But for some reason, as his hand touched metal and embedded jewels, the feel of the egg didn't seem as much like magic this morning. It wasn't warm. It wasn't electric to the touch as it sometimes had been.

Chase heard a noise, forgot the egg and looked up to find the source. The buzzing sound of a small motor off in the distance made him turn his head. He saw that the noise was coming from a riding mower.

Unbidden thoughts of Kate suddenly drifted through his mind. With a mild jolt, he also realized that the egg's metal under his fingers was now heating up. But why?

As if he had somehow conjured up the vision, the

noisy riding mower came closer and the person in the driver's seat could be clearly seen. It was Kate.

He shook his head and nearly laughed out loud. Princess Kate? On a riding mower? Her father would never have allowed such a thing.

Kate waved, stopped the mower about twenty feet away and stepped off. "Isn't Shelby around? I thought she would be here to show you in." Kate began walking toward him.

"She was here when I arrived," he muttered. "Showed me around the house and gave me a key."

Chase moved to the edge of the veranda and towered above the previous mistress of the house. "I didn't believe her when she said you were outside doing chores. It's a good thing I saw it for myself."

Using her hand to shelter her eyes from the bright sun, Kate smiled up at him. "There are many things you need to see for yourself, *cher.*"

The seduction in her voice and the clearly sensual look in her gaze caught him off guard. All of the indecision and conflicted feelings about Kate bubbled up to the surface just to tantalize him.

Annoyed with himself for not being able to control his desires, he spoke much too harshly. "I can afford to hire out the yard work. No need to use my hands for such things."

"I like using my hands for many fine things," she told him with a sensual edge to her voice.

Her skin glistened with sweat in the hot sun as she stood defiantly and watched him. Chase's annoyance turned to furious need in an instant.

Dammit. And damn her.

Once Kate had been simple to understand and his desperate desire for her was easy and straightforward. Then, while he'd been away, the memory of Kate had turned to pure pain, stark and bitter in its cold reality.

What the hell was he supposed to feel about her now? Who was this Kate? Was she the one who had turned her back on him and everything they had together? Or was this the stranger Kate? One who had taken in Shelby and the baby.

"Come inside, Chase. I'll fix us something icy to drink before I make you feel at home."

The obvious innuendo did nothing but irritate him. He gritted his teeth and scowled.

"Go clean up, *chère*," he muttered. "You're filthy. Your father would be turning over in his grave." He pulled the car keys from his jeans pocket. "I have things to do. Don't expect me back until late."

"But, Chase…"

Striding past her with as much force as possible, Chase closed his heart to her soft sighs. This was too difficult.

He had to get away before she stole the last of his control. Being near her had just become impossible to bear.

# Six

Kate imagined herself to be a ghost—the dead mistress of the plantation manor, standing on the dimly lit landing at the top of the stairs awaiting the lover that would never return.

This was *so* not what she should be doing. Obviously, she'd been reading way too many romance novels.

Sitting down in the straight-backed chair she'd dragged out to the landing overlooking the entry foyer, Kate chided herself for being so melodramatic. Having a good chuckle at her own expense was a lot smarter than having a good cry because Chase hadn't come back to Live Oak Hall yet today.

Was it possible she'd talked herself into believing that he wanted her every bit as badly as she wanted him? Maybe. Because she wanted him bad. But the fire in his eyes whenever he looked her way matched hers exactly. And his need seemed plain enough.

When she'd asked what he wanted that first night out on the B&B's terrace, he'd said it was her, hadn't he? So what was stopping him?

Over this long day of wondering where Chase had gone and when he would be back, Kate had made up a half-dozen reasons why he might not want to have an affair with her. Right at the top of the list was the idea that the rumors were true and that she really had become a frigid, unattractive spinster. Every single man she'd dated since Chase had left town had complained that she was cold and off-putting.

Kate had wondered if what they'd said might be true. Right up until Chase came back to town. Absolutely sure the gossip was wrong now, she marveled at all her renewed heat. With erotic and steamy passion blasting through the air whenever the two of them came together, she had never felt so hot in her entire life.

Maybe Chase's hesitance came from his continuing anger at her for turning her back on him all those years ago. His old wounds might be keeping him from recognizing the sensual pull that existed between them now. Kate frowned at the very thought.

How would she convince him to help the town and the mill if he wouldn't let her get too close? And how would she quiet her own furious desire to get him into bed if he refused her touch?

Kate swiped at her eyes, willing the tears away. Just this morning she had vowed never to be a coward again. To let nothing stop her from going for what she wanted.

Well…she wanted Chase. Not for the long term, of

course. That was a schoolgirl's dream she'd given up on the night he'd left town for good.

No, she wanted him for a short-term affair. A fiery and passionate few weeks when they wouldn't have to talk about the past—or maybe when they wouldn't have to talk about anything *at all* during eternal nights of mindless sex.

That was the reason she had dressed in this flimsy negligee, a black lace reminder of richer times…and now sat here in half darkness waiting for him to come back. Somehow she would find a way to show Chase that they could be lovers without recriminations. That they could simply take pleasure in each other's bodies and forget the rest.

Through the stillness of the night, Kate heard his car roaring up the allée toward the house. Finally. It must be long past midnight.

The noise of the engine switched off and she found herself holding her breath, waiting for him to come through the door. But endless silence dragged on and on, forcing her to eventually breathe—and to pray.

"Come on in, *cher,*" she urged him in her mind. "I will make it worth your while. I promise."

But ten minutes later Chase had still not come through the front door. Kate decided she'd better go see what was wrong. Perhaps his key would not work in the lock.

Disregarding her state of undress, Kate sneaked quietly down the stairs and inched open the front door. A full, blue moon illuminated the veranda so that it was much brighter outside than it was inside the house.

She was out the door before she even spotted Chase, sitting in one of the antique rockers a couple of yards down on the veranda. His eyelids were closed and he looked like a man asleep.

"Chase, why haven't you come inside to bed?" she whispered, quite sure that he was not really asleep.

Slowly he opened his eyes and gazed up at her with a lazy, languid stare. "I didn't want to disturb you, *chère*. I'm comfortable here and wanted to make sure you were asleep before I came inside."

"Um…" She inched farther out into the brilliant moonlight. "Will we be sleeping in the same bed tonight? I thought we could move into the old master suite—my grandparent's bedroom. It has a big queen-size bed. I made it up with clean sheets and…"

"No, Kate," he said with a low growl. "Go to bed by yourself. We will not be sleeping together."

"But why not?" she demanded, already feeling slightly hysterical. "I thought you said you wanted me. What changed?"

Chase rocked back into a shadow so she couldn't see his expression. The damn man had a habit of doing that, and it was driving her crazy not being able to see his eyes.

Out of the darkness he whispered, "I won't have sex with someone whose only motivation is to bribe me to get what she wants.

"You look cold in that sheer scrap of nothing," he continued gruffly. "Trying to prove the word going around about you is true? Cold-fish Kate? Go crawl into your own nice warm bed and leave me alone to freeze by myself."

"But that's not true…"

"You mean this cold attempt at seduction isn't meant solely to convince me to bring the mill back to its old glory?"

"No," she hedged, suddenly far more desperate than she should be. "I can't say that isn't part of it…but the mill's not everything."

"What else is there, *chère?* I've already said Shelby and the baby can stay as long as they need to. You can stay, too. But not in my bed."

Kate was on the verge of a full-blown panic. She wanted to scream at him that what she needed were his lips and his hands on her greedy body. She'd dreamed of his caresses for so very long.

Chase couldn't possibly mean that he was not interested at all. Even from this distance and not being able to see his eyes through the pitch-black darkness, Kate could feel the tension growing between them. At this moment she didn't care if he helped bring the mill back or not—but she did care a lot about getting him to touch her again.

He wanted her. She was positive that he did. And she was determined to make him see just how much.

In her bare feet, Kate tiptoed closer to the edge of the veranda, making sure she was clearly visible to Chase in the yellow glow of moonlight. Then turning to face him straight-on, she spread her legs and planted her feet for balance.

"I have dreamed of being with you, Chase. For ten lonely years my body has ached for your touch."

He made no comment, and she almost went into the shadows to shake sense into him. Vowing to shake him up from a distance instead, Kate took off her silky robe and dropped it to the veranda floor. Which left her in nothing but a see-through nightgown.

"I don't expect you to care about me," she told him

boldly. "That's not necessary. And I certainly don't expect any promises—for anything."

Taking another breath, Kate wiggled out of the long nightgown and let it pool around her bare feet. The shock of the cool night air ran goose bumps over her body. She knew he was watching her, and her breasts were suddenly full and achy. The heat quickly spread across her chest and moved lower, doing away with the bumps and bringing moist sweat to secret spots instead.

She was standing scandalously naked before him and still he said nothing.

But she could feel his eyes on her body—the same way they had been over the strip poker game—the same way they had been under the willow when the two of them were young and desperate.

Kate knew she had his full attention. And she intended to force him to fold. He would not be able to keep his distance after she showed him the power of her hand in this risky game.

Hands. She arched her back and ran her hands up her rib cage until they cupped her breasts.

If she'd had enough nerve to play strip poker with him, she certainly could go the extra mile tonight. He liked to watch. Okay then. She would give him something to watch.

Lifting one breast up far enough so that the stiff peak would be clearly visible, Kate used her own fingers to roll and pinch the sensitive nipple. "This is what I want from you," she said with a small groan. "It has nothing to do with the mill. If I close my eyes, I can pretend it's your fingers on my skin again after all this time."

She leaned back against a solid oak post and let her

eyelids drift down. Then she licked the fingers of her other hand and tugged at the second nipple until it too became purple and engorged.

· "I can dream that my hand is your mouth, tasting, laving, drawing me up unmercifully." The bolts of electricity had begun to run from her breasts to other spots on her body that begged for his attention. "Can you taste me still, *cher?* After all these years, I remember. Do you?"

From out of the darkness, she heard him take a ragged breath, and it spurred her on. Gave her courage.

As she ran a hand lightly down her abdomen and inched toward the tender spot between her thighs, Kate's body began to react to the touches. Even if they were just from her own hands.

Lifting a foot and letting it rest on a low bench beside her, Kate felt the shock of night air as the breeze palmed her in the most private area. She wanted Chase to clearly see what she was doing to herself. What she wanted him to do to her instead.

"All those years apart, Chase. All those desolate nights. I dreamed of you touching me…taking me. I learned that I could make-believe that it was you inside me." She slid her fingers through the tangled nest of her own curls, heading lower.

"I imagined your tongue opening my secret folds, your hot breath on me as you nibbled and teased the very heart of my passion." She sucked two fingers into her mouth, getting them completely wet.

Giving herself permission to do whatever gave the most pleasure, she groaned aloud. Then she slipped one lubricated finger inside the tender spot at the juncture of her legs. The place that was pulsing and ready to be stroked.

"I learned how to do the same things you had done to me so long ago." Her voice had grown raspy, hoarse with frustrating passion. "I imagined how to think of you and touch myself in just the right way."

She used the other wet finger to tickle the sensitive nub at the entrance to her core. And found that it was raw with desire and begging for attention. The sensations she created with her fingers caused her breath to come in short pants. Waves of pleasure began building deep and low in her belly, urging her to hurry up and finish the discussion so Chase could take over.

"Do you see, Chase? Do you see what thoughts of you can do? I want you here inside of me. I want the real thing. I want…"

The shocking words she'd uttered were suddenly interrupted by moaning cries—as her orgasm snuck up and engulfed her. She'd let herself get too close. Chase hadn't made a move.

But at that same moment she heard Chase's hiss of surprise and desire coming out of the shadows. Too late.

Then all she could hear was heavy breathing as circles of climax swamped her body in liquid heat and blazing insanity. Wetness covered her hand, her legs shook violently, and the world disappeared in a slick sensual mist.

Light-headed and limp, Kate began sinking to her knees as she lowered herself against the post. She'd messed up. She had come too soon and her chance at convincing Chase to come with her was gone for good.

But in her next lucid moment, she found Chase kneeling beside her. *"C'est impossible,"* he groaned as he lifted her into his arms. "I can no longer deny that I want you. The sight of you has driven me to madness. You are my obsession. You always have been. I don't care if you are the echo of past mistakes. I must have you."

His mouth came down on hers with such a frantic demand that she cried out in shock. But the hard pressure of his mouth switched her cries of surprise to moans of erotic pleasure in an instant.

Her mouth opened under his and their tongues tangled, creating brand-new delicious tingles in her lower body. She was aware of his hard, muscled chest, his strength and his masculinity. And she was instantly ready again, wanting him savagely—right now.

Chase never took his mouth from hers, but pushed through the front doors with Kate still in his arms as he headed toward the stairs. He broke the kiss long enough to bound up the staircase.

"Front left room, right?" he gasped at the landing.

"Huh?" she gulped, incapable of comprehension.

"The master suite."

"Oh. Yes." Finally. Wonderfully. "Yes. Hurry."


Gypsy Passionata Chagari skulked back into the shadows of Blackwater Bayou and watched as the river snakes glided past, through tea-colored waters.

"At last you make your move, young Severin," she mumbled to herself with great irritation. "But you do so with a grudge in your heart."

She flicked her wrist and swore. "You strain my patience, Severin. I have come to you, knowing your irreverence and disbelief would test the magic. Now you force my hand."

Folding her arms over her chest, Passionata began to pace through cypress knees and vine-tangled ankle-deep swamp. What could she do to open his eyes to the truth? This young gambler refused to accept what was placed in front of him. To him, all hands were bluffs.

Reckless young man.

"Well, you have met your match with me," she vowed. "My family owes your family the magic and you will accept. You have no choice."

Grumbling those words aloud reminded her of the origin of the debt owed by the family Chagari to the Steele family. Life. The ultimate magic.

That was the answer, she thought with a smile. She eased a hand into her pocket and pulled out the crystal.

"You escape the truth no longer, Severin. You've been hiding from life itself, wrapped up in old, imagined injuries, licking at wounds that never existed."

Passionata lifted her arm in a wide arch across the crystal, conjuring up the magic. "I will not allow you to hide this time. You must face life head-on before you can learn to embrace it and accept your destiny."

Smoke flew from her fingers. Lightning lit up the clear midnight sky. "I give to you the ultimate magic, young heir to Lucille Steele. I give to you a second chance to grasp the dream. This time you will be forced to accept your destiny."

Kate was beyond his dreams, Chase thought briefly as he lowered her to the bed and began to strip off his clothes. After all these years, he'd forgotten the way her voice turned to silk and wound lazily around his libido.

He hadn't remembered how responsive to every touch she was…or how easily she flamed.

Heaven help him. He would never in a million years forget it again. The sight of her trembling and naked on the veranda in the moonlight would remain with him forever—right on the edge of his sanity.

He still didn't know who she really was—but for now he didn't care. For now he would take—and give— as much bodily pleasure as he could manage.

But he did know that the heat and the need were just wisps of shadowy fog, obscuring reality. And he would not soon forget about that, either.

He stepped out of his jeans and tossed them aside with his shirt. Looming over Kate as she lay on her back and gazed up at him, Chase tried to recapture a little control. If he did what his body demanded, he would have her now and take what he desired without a thought to her needs.

Like hell. He owed her nothing, but every fiber in his body screamed for him to go slow. Tease her, bring her to the brink again and again the way she had tried to do to him.

And in the meantime, he would be satisfying himself as well. He would test the taste of her to see if she lived up to his memories. He would touch every tender spot that he remembered, perhaps finding new ones as he went along.

Groaning, he bent over her and, taking her chin in his hand, forced her to look him in the eyes. "It's my turn to see how far we can push each other, *chère*. You are under my spell now. I will decide when it's time for you to go over, and when it is time for you suffer as you balance on the edge of oblivion.

"You've asked for everything you will receive…and more," he finished in a harsh whisper.

Chase had meant to shake her up, stop her from being so complacent in the knowledge that she could drive him insane just by watching. He needed to make her anticipate the sensual waves to come.

But instead of caution, all he saw in those demon black eyes were smiles of womanly desire. She lowered her lashes and ran her tongue over her bottom lip—and he swore silently to himself.

*Damn her.* With a swift movement that surprised even him, Chase grabbed both of her wrists and imprisoned them above her head with one hand. In a sudden frenzy, his lips descended on hers, demanding a fiery response.

And he got it. Her whole body jerked, arched upward while she rubbed herself against his naked chest. She nipped and licked at his lips as she writhed with pleasure.

*Damn her.* He refused to give up this much control.

Trying to stand his ground and drive her even crazier, Chase covered one breast with his free hand and deviled the beaded tip with his fingers. Then tearing his lips from hers, he bent nearly double and sucked the other nipple into his mouth.

"Chase," she cried. "Take me." Her feet kicked out as she wrapped her legs around his hips and pressed herself to his hardened length.

*Damn her.* He was losing it. The sound of her violent passion shoved him right to the edge. But he held on, determined to be in control. What had happened to his promises to drive her insane?

He'd wanted a slow torture. He'd wanted to take the

time to linger. To taste and excite. To savor the flavors of Kate. Now all of that would have to come another time.

*Damn her.* It was beyond his power to push her away and slow things down. Something drove him on with thoughtless abandon. He slid his hand between them and found her hot and wet, as ready for their joining as he was.

Letting go of her wrists, he eased back to look at her. She blinked and smiled up at him. God, she was a picture. Her whole body was inflamed, the breasts full and the nipples bright rose and peaked. Her eyes were deep, dark pools. Her skin glistened with musky sweat.

He craved a taste. Chase put a fingertip to the tiny bud at the entrance to her core, dipped inside and pulled the finger back, sucking it into his mouth.

Kate squeaked and scrambled out from under him before he could stop her. "Wait…*wait,*" she sobbed. "Hold on."

In a flurry of motion, she jerked open the drawer of a side table and pulled out a foil packet. Shaking violently, she ripped at the packet with her teeth. In the next instant, Kate tried to touch him, tried to cover him.

But as close as he was to oblivion, he couldn't let her try. He took care of it himself as she lay back on the bed and opened her legs.

"Please hurry, Chase," she moaned, her voice hushed and breathless.

*Damn her.* Those had been his thoughts exactly. That is, if you could call what was going on in his mind thinking.

He slid his hand under her bottom and lifted her to meet him. Then in one gloriously long stoke, he thrust inside. Both of them shuddered, crazed by the pure pleasure in their joining.

Tight, warm and welcoming, Kate was everything he'd ever wanted. He stilled for one second just to let himself enjoy. With another little squeak, she tilted her hips higher and he slid in deeper. It was the end of thinking.

Frantic stroke after frantic stroke drove the two of them to new heights. He was drenched in sweat, but he'd stopped feeling anything save for the furious need building to unbearable heights. His muscles flexed and bunched as he pumped, met her hips, drew back and dove in with more force.

Kate was sobbing, begging for release and moaning with pleasure. *Kate,* was the only thing he could hear repeating in his mind. His Kate—home at last.

When her internal muscles began to clutch at him in the same way her fingers were digging into his arms, Chase let himself go. With an exquisite and continuous surge of rippling completion, Chase topped the cliff just as he heard her groaning his name aloud.

In his mind the refrain repeated over and over.

Kate. Kate. Why has it been so long?

*Damn her.* And damn himself for so easily ignoring everything else.

# Seven

Chase rolled to his side and sat upright on the edge of the bed with his back to her. He scrubbed a hand across his mouth.

*Et là,* he swore silently. Stunned by what had taken place between them, he fought for breath and focus. He'd been gob-smacked. Someone had apparently scrambled his brains with a two-by-four.

The Kate he remembered from his boyhood had been sensual and responsive. The grown-up Kate was all that and so much more. He'd wanted her tonight in a way that he had never before wanted anything or anyone. With a blindness that bordered on compulsion.

He'd called her an obsession. Ha! Little did he know what a mild word that would be for the forces sizzling between them.

"Hell, Kate," he managed without looking at her. "That wasn't the way tonight was supposed to go."

"No?" He heard the sated and purely feminine lilt in her voice. "I thought it went extremely well."

He stood, slipped into the bathroom and pitched the condom, all in a desperate effort to keep his distance from her. Raking the fingers of one hand through his hair as he returned to the bed, Chase grumbled, "Smug, aren't you?"

Irritated at his own stupidity in being swept away by a woman he shouldn't trust, Chase gritted his teeth and tried to think of a good way to make her back off. He wasn't sure he could be strong enough to walk away from her tonight, even though that *should* be his only choice. So he had to find a way to make Kate go first.

"What's the town's ice princess doing with a stash of condoms in her nightstand, *chère?*" It wasn't a gentlemanly thing to ask, but it had been bugging him…almost as much as the building rage to be inside her once more.

He could've sworn he'd caught a flash of pain in her dark eyes before she smiled shyly and said, "I found an old box of them stuffed in the back of a bathroom drawer. It kinda gives me the creeps thinking they must've once been my father's, but the box had never been opened so I refuse to consider the possibilities."

"Still running from the truth, Kate?" He shot her his best sneer.

But he nearly choked on his own tongue when her face contorted with anguish. Dammit. He'd pushed too hard.

Blindsided and stung as if Chase had hit her, Kate moved off the bed and headed toward the bathroom. She could've sworn there had been magic between them a few minutes ago. Now all she wanted to do was get away from him and hide.

Damn him.

But she hadn't even made it three feet before she felt his firm grip on her arm, slowing her steps and turning her around to face him.

"Kate," he said on a breath. "Forgive me. I was feeling cornered, like I'd lost my free will. Like someone was pulling invisible strings to make me do things I had no intention of doing. Maybe we rushed into sex too fast."

*Cornered?* By her? That was such a backward idea it was almost laughable. But she didn't feel much like laughing. She still craved him, her body hadn't stopped throbbing for him. And damned if she was just going to let him shove her away when they clearly had something so incredible together.

She steadied herself, stepped closer and felt the heat radiating from his body. "Chase," she said on a sigh. "Our past will forever come between us and make a future impossible, I know that. I wasn't trying to corner you tonight. There has never been anyone in my bed except you, I swear. So I'm not on the Pill or anything.

"I just wanted us to take pleasure in each other for the moment," she continued. "It wasn't a deliberate plan. It was simply our needs that made us both lose control."

He looked uncertain and his hesitancy ripped at her gut, clutched at her soul.

"Admit there's enough tension between us to light up the entire state," she insisted. Her tone of voice was getting higher with frustration. "I'm not looking for forever…I know that's not a possibility. But couldn't we just forget the past long enough to enjoy what we have while we can?"

"You don't care what kind of scandal that might cause in this town?" he asked with a frown. "The former ice princess being the mistress of the poor kid who hit it rich and came back to own it all?"

The word *scandal* should've stopped her, slowed her down to think of the consequences of what she was asking. But it didn't. Not in the least. She didn't give a roaring rip about what the town thought of her anymore.

If she'd taken time to consider her newly discovered freedom from guilt for very long, the irony of it might've given her pause. But as badly as she wanted to touch Chase again, there was nothing that could stand in her way.

She took another step closer and raised her hand to lightly caress his chest. Dying to stroke his skin, run her hands through his hair and force him back into her bed, Kate still felt startled as his muscles jumped under her fingers.

He captured her hand with his own and held it to his thumping heart. "It's obviously no secret that you turn me on. What we just did… How you make me feel…"

He left the thought hanging, and she saw the conflict in his eyes. "It was incredible," he finally whispered. "Beyond anything. No woman has ever…"

Shaking his head, Chase seemed to be in a huge battle within himself. "There are many things left that I still dream of doing…to you…with you."

She moaned and reached out to touch his jutting manhood with her free hand. But he grabbed her wrist with a steel-edged grip and kept her still.

"Be sure in your mind that this arrangement will be only temporary, *chère*," he growled. "Who is going to say when it's over?"

The stab of regret she'd felt when he mentioned the end was thankfully fleeting. Kate wanted him badly enough to do anything. Say anything.

"*You* will," she answered forcefully. "You don't even have to tell me when to go. When you no longer want me, I'll know. And I'll leave on my own."

For several frozen moments, Chase's gaze drifted to her mouth, lingered and grew impossibly hot. But then all of sudden, he issued a sound that seemed more animal than human, grabbed her up and launched them both back on to the mattress.

Chase rolled her on her back and covered her body with his own. Seeking her mouth, he kissed her hard. As he ground his hips into hers, everything became mind-blanking passion and lust-filled energy.

She squirmed and arched under him, seeking an elusive quenching for this terrible thirst. Instead of giving her what she craved, though, Chase broke the kiss, stilled and leaned up on his elbows to gaze down at her face.

"No, *chère*," he murmured as his pewter eyes searched hers. "There will be no rushing for us."

When she began to whimper in protest, he gave her a devilishly cocky smile and touched a finger to her lips. "Shh, Kate. We have all night." He captured her gaze and held her mesmerized in his spell.

He slid the pad of his thumb lightly over her bottom lip. She felt the tension growing in her gut and—much lower. Her legs automatically opened beneath him, the movement seeming to make his shaft grow harder against her belly where their bodies came together.

"I love your mouth, *chère*," he told her seductively. He slanted his head, nipped at her bottom lip and sucked it into his.

She heard herself moan. He lifted his head just enough to grin down at her. "Slow and steady is the way. Everything will be more vivid, more enjoyable. You feeling it yet, Kate?"

She couldn't answer. And could only groan and clutch at his shoulders.

He inched backward down her body, kissing a path along her neck and across her chest as he went. "Easy, *chère*. Let the sensations take you. Take us both."

Chase rubbed one of her beaded and distended nipples between his fingers. The jolt zinged along her nerve endings.

"Chase. Please," she gasped.

"Hmm. Yeah." He hummed low and deep within his chest. Staring longingly down at her, once again he sat back and watched as both her peaks jutted forward and begged for attention.

It was crystal clear to her now why he always watched her from the shadows. The hunger in his eyes gave him away.

"We will please each other later. But for now…"

Swift and sure enough to drive her to madness, Chase ran his tongue across one throbbing nub. Pulling back, he lightly blew over her skin until she moaned again. The shock of his heated breath, mixing with the cold air, made Kate positive she would soon explode.

"For now…I please myself." He bent his head and

placed a gentle kiss on her other neglected but puckered nipple.

Laving, nipping lightly and then kissing each tip, Chase's movements were driving erotic electricity down her spine. Tiny red ants must've slipped into her arteries because the fire inflamed her from the inside out.

It was too difficult to be teased like this without completion, she thought distractedly. Kate liked her sex with Chase to be quick and fast. Hot and wild.

But she nearly changed her mind when the delight of his clever tongue, drawing lazy circles over her sensitive skin, sent a shudder humming through her body. Still, Kate's conscious mind fought the slow tempo.

Taking pleasure in this long, drawn-out and tantalizing manner meant she would also have plenty of time to think. To wonder if they would be doing these same sorts of things next week. Next month.

Kate wasn't sure she could hold herself together well enough to keep him until tomorrow, let alone to next month. Every minute they were intimate brought her closer to dreaming of a future that would never be. A few more weeks of this, and she might be lost for good.

Things between them had already advanced past simple remembered passion and into something much more complicated. She didn't dare let herself get too wrapped up in him again. When he left this time it might be the end of her entirely.

As if he knew of her simmering anguish, he murmured against her skin, "Stop thinking and give in, *chère*. Lie back and go with the flow. Let yourself feel. Let me take you to the next place."

She shivered as if in the throes of a raging fever. Hot

then cold. Logical then incoherent. Wanting to drive him up this same ledge along with her, Kate swept her hands along his back then fisted them in his hair. The silken feel of him made her ache unbearably.

Chase eased off the bed and stood looming above her, watching. She writhed and moaned, holding out her arms to bring him closer. But he pushed her arms aside as he began to trace his fingertip down an invisible line, starting between her breasts and moving lower.

When he reached a spot right below her belly button, Chase hesitated, ignoring the pulsing hidden place that longed for his attention. Instead of continuing downward, he tenderly laid both his hands flat against her abdomen and took a deep breath. The look in his eyes was full of promise, and the tension coiled ever tighter inside her.

At last he let his hands glide erotically down her hips and lower, until his touch warmed and shocked her sensitive inner thighs. Her hips jerked and she grew wetter, wilder.

Suddenly the sensations were too intense, too carnal. It made her realize that she'd merely been existing for the last ten years of her life. There could never be anyone else she would want to touch her in this way. Only Chase. Only him.

The throbbing between her legs and the hunger in her belly was beyond imagining. She moaned, flailed her arms and legs and cried out. "Chase!"

Smiling at her desperation, he knelt beside her on the bed, bent over and replaced his palms with his lips. It was torture as he kissed her thighs, licking his way ever higher. It made her whole body shudder…tremble with anticipation. She lost all sense of reason.

Groaning and sobbing his name, she reached out to touch him in an intimate way. She ran her fingers lightly up and down his shaft, testing and marveling at the moisture on the tip. Then she gently palmed the tender skin beneath his erection.

His warm, wet responses to her touch made her hotter, as he grew ever thicker under her ministrations. She closed her hand around him, reveling in the hardness covered over by such tender silk. So male.

When he moved his body slightly so he could be in a better position to put his mouth against the nub at her core, Kate scooted under his knee, lining herself up directly under him. He opened the tender lips between her legs with gentle fingers and kissed her in the most intimate place.

"Chase. Oh, Chase." Only him. Only this man. Forever.

She lifted her hips to meet his tongue. At the same time, she arched up, taking his erection into her mouth. Both of them quivered at the shock of such exquisite pleasure. Then, together they moaned with savage abandon as each licked, sucked and explored the other at will.

Kate felt an explosion building right at the edge of her consciousness and dug her heels into the bedding. Waiting. Expecting.

It was too much. She couldn't breathe. Knew she could never make the wonder of this last.

In the next instant, though, Chase's whole body jumped as if he'd been hit. He clamored away from her.

"I want to be inside you," he gasped. "I can't… I'm too close." In three fast-as-lightning moves, Chase ripped open the drawer, fitted himself with another condom and flipped them both back on the bed, with her landing on top.

Impatient, Kate groaned with a noise that sounded savage and wild. She straddled him, then leaned heavily across Chase's chest and nipped at one of his nipples with her teeth. The pressure curled in her chest, and she moaned past her dry, constricted throat.

Chase arched and eased just his tip inside her body.

She wanted all of him, buried deep and right now. Expecting him to surge up and drive his shaft to the very hilt, Kate paused. Instead, she felt Chase still. He had hold of her hips, keeping her steady and caught between heaven and hell. Scraping her nails down his chest in frustration, she raised her head and glared at him.

His nostrils flared, the veins corded in his neck. "You know what I want," he moaned. "But you need to lead the way this time. Take charge, *chère*. It's your move." He took his hands from her hips, waiting for her.

All of sudden she recognized what he was doing. He had turned over complete control. He'd put her in the position of power, forcing a decision on what would give them both the most fulfillment. She could pick up the pace, slow it down or quit altogether.

Ohmigod. No one had ever deliberately given her so much control—over what happened, over herself—never in her entire lifetime.

Always in her past, she'd had to sneak around to get what she wanted. Sometimes she'd begged. Sometimes she'd lied. Other times she'd had to coax, like she'd done with Chase earlier tonight on the veranda.

But now here she was, free to make a choice openly. For the very first time in her life. And of all people in the universe, it would have to be Chase who had elevated her status in this way.

She wasn't too sure why he'd done it. But it was clear that he was the only one whose gift of control could've meant so much.

Blinking back tears, Kate made her move. She eased her hips down and took him a little deeper.

Chase groaned. Kate heard herself chuckle at his need, enjoying her new power game. She watched his face and saw the wildness and frustration of holding back, gleaming in his stainless-steel eyes.

"I thought you liked taking things slow," she teased.

He reached up and palmed her nipples, kneading, begging with just a touch. "You're killing me here," he moaned in a husky, on-the-verge-of-losing-it voice that surprised her.

Bending double, Chase took one of her achy peaks into his mouth and suckled hard. It sent Kate right over the edge. She quickly gave up her new control as the sensual lust-filled haze captured them both in tender talons. Control stopped mattering.

Slow became fast. Torment became gratification.

Kate jammed down hard and sat straight up, taking him fully inside her body. Chase gasped. His breathing started coming in short staccato bursts.

His hips jerked and surged higher, intensifying the pleasure for both of them. She raised up slowly then slammed back down, matching him thrust for thrust.

She tried to keep her eyes trained on his face as the pressure inside built to bursting. But as both of them grew slick with sweat, their eyes glazed over with need. Lost in the moment, the two were completely oblivious to the sounds of their own primitive howls of mating.

Too soon, but unable to hold it back, Kate closed her eyes and arched, letting the overpowering climax take over. Her internal muscles clenched around his erection and she relished each squeeze. Wave after glorious wave dashed them on a precious shoreline.

She felt Chase's climax explode as he threw back his head and roared. He reached up, pulled her into a tight embrace and dragged her down against his chest. Together they circled on and on in a crazy whirlpool…rushing toward a more dangerous place than they had ever been before.

When Chase finally managed to breathe normally again, he rolled to one side, taking Kate with him. He tucked her close to his body. When she snuggled in and her whole body relaxed against him, he was floored by how vulnerable he felt.

He stared up at the ceiling and had a flash of that same gut-punching need he'd experienced the night of their strip poker game. As hot for her as he still was at the moment, his body's overriding mandate seemed to be geared more toward protection. To keep her safe and warm in the circle of his embrace.

Son of a… Why?

Kate hadn't been the wronged person in their past relationship. She had betrayed *him*. Lied and schemed to get him out of town. He shouldn't trust her at all. She could obviously protect herself.

But the niggle of a memory long forgotten pushed at his conscious mind. He didn't want to think back to their youth. Especially not now. He didn't want to face the humiliation and anger he'd felt back then—ever again.

Want to or not, the question about her motives latched on and refused to be dismissed. Why had she wanted him to leave town badly enough to lie to the sheriff about what had happened that night?

He'd been so angry and so emotionally injured for the last ten years that he'd refused to think about her motives. Now he couldn't stop thinking of them. What good had it done her to send him out of town in that particular way?

If she'd been the spoiled little rich girl he thought he'd known, she could've just as easily put her nose in the air, told him they were finished and then walked away without all the melodramatics.

Kate moaned beside him and pressed her lips to his neck, bringing his mind out of the past and back to the present with a rock-hard thud.

Her breath was soft and sultry as she whispered against his skin, "Is it still my turn to control things? If so…"

She reached out, closing her fingers around his immediately hardened erection. He hissed, sucked in air and forced himself to repack the baggage of yesteryear. He willed his mind to forget about everything—except the here and now.

Chase surrendered to the furious need to be one with her once more. There was a vague feeling of danger, pulsing inside him and urging him to name the terms of their affair. But he didn't care.

Sudden hunger raged, demanding to be set free. His heartbeat raced. When Kate pulled his head to her breast, begging him to suckle, his mind went totally blank. Without words, she was pleading with him to stir their shared passion to the boiling point again.

He decided to answer the question first. "It's still your choice, *chère*. What do you want?"

Kate shrieked with delight and twisted beneath him. "Hot and fast," she insisted with fervor.

Chase gave in to the haunting fury howling for release inside him. Grabbing both her wrists, he dragged them over her head and pushed into her body on one long, fast thrust.

She called his name with a whimper and begged with a smile. Chase gladly complied as he swung her knees over his shoulders, going straight to the depths of where he'd longed to be.

Her heartbeat drummed a steady beat in his ears. Her sighs of pleasure sounded a loud demand in his soul.

Taking another breath, he let the familiar scent of her play havoc with his senses. *His* Kate. His everything.

They joined together throughout the night, behaving as though they were one sole entity. Reaching for each other over and over, they gave no thought to what their joining might mean. Or to what price would have to be paid for ignoring the lessons of the past.

But off in the swamp, on a midnight-black wind, the gypsy knew. And she welcomed it.

# Eight

With her hair pulled back in a tightly wound ponytail, Kate wielded the spatula in the same way a swashbuckler might thrust his rapier. Shaking her head and cussing under her breath, she wondered how on earth Shelby ever managed to control the ancient stove that inhabited the plantation's kitchen.

Kate seldom did any cooking, but today she had awoken in a domesticated and homey mood. And making breakfast for Chase seemed like just the right thing to do.

But the pancakes she'd been attempting kept burning around the edges, even as their batter remained uncooked in the middle. *Et là,* she swore. Giving up, she threw out that batch and poured another. What would a sunny Sunday morning be without pancakes?

No matter whatever else she did, Kate's mind refused to stay focused on the job at hand. Her head was swimming with images of a sensual night with Chase.

Erotic daydreams filled the corners of her mind—quite pleasantly. She couldn't believe that she was really going to be Chase's mistress. Even if her days with him would be limited, every fantasy she'd had for ten years was finally coming true.

She vaguely remembered that as a teenager he'd been a patient and tender lover. Whoo boy. He was so far beyond that now it was incredible. Their bodies responded to each other with breathless passion. And they fit together as if they'd been built from heavenly specifications designed explicitly for mating.

Erotic visions of his urgent touches and echoes of his scandalous whispers pushed aside her usual good sense. They struck a blow, as well, to all those other subconscious warnings of impending disaster that she should've been heeding. Kate was slowly being stripped of normal inhibitions, leaving her wide open and way too vulnerable.

Oh, back in the furthest reaches of her mind, she knew that to him this was all just sex. And just temporary sex, at that. Soon enough Chase would make a final decision about the mill and then he would be gone. Off to the next casino or business in need of new management.

Kate felt fairly confident that she would be able to live through his leaving this time. She'd managed to keep on going through her devastation the last time around—and through much worse, too. But this time, although she was so much stronger now, Kate wouldn't have her home and family business to fall back on. And after last night, she wondered if she would ever be able to get another full night's sleep without being cradled in Chase's arms.

Sighing, she caught the faint whiff of something burning and looked down at the pancakes, curling black around the edges on the grill. Damn.

"Making charcoal, *chère?*"

She jerked, swore and dropped one of the pancakes on the floor. Glaring over her shoulder at Chase standing in the doorway, Kate watched as he moved toward her with a bemused look on his face.

"Five-second rule applies," he said with a grin. Grabbing the spatula from her hand, he flipped the pancake off the floor and back onto the griddle.

"Chase, what on earth…"

Shoving his hip into hers, he nudged her aside and began flipping pancakes like a pro. "The heat will kill any germs. Set the table, Kate. These will be done in a second."

"You know how to cook pancakes?" She stepped over to the silverware drawer but sneaked a look back at him.

This morning he had dressed in sexy, light-blue jeans and a work shirt with its long sleeves rolled halfway up his arms. The muscles on his forearms bulged as he worked. His wonderful chestnut hair was dark and wet from a shower, and he smelled like citrus aftershave.

Her hunger turned from food to more erotic pursuits in a flash.

"Of course I can cook," he told her with a smirk. "To manage employees properly, you should be able to do every job in the joint. Since I own and run both casinos and restaurants, I know how to cook, deal cards, reset the slot machines, purchase supplies…even wash the dishes."

He flipped a couple of pancakes onto a plate and handed it to her. "You hungry?"

She was, but not for food. He looked good enough to eat this morning, and that image was blinding her to anything else.

Chase poured a couple more pancakes out on the griddle. "Go ahead and start without me," he urged when she just stood there watching him. "Don't want yours to get cold. The next ones will be done in a minute, anyway."

Sitting down at the table, she kept her eyes trained on his back. He was so spectacular. Efficient, not afraid of a little work and sexy as hell.

A tiny bud of hope sprang in her breast. Maybe if she told him the truth of what happened that night ten years ago, he would be able to forgive her. Then she might have a chance of remaining his mistress, no matter where he went from here.

Surely Chase would admit that the sex between them was better than just good. In fact, somewhere in the mist of the erotic haze that had wiped her mind clean last night, she remembered him saying something exactly like that.

Calculating her chances for success at getting his forgiveness, she decided to find just the right time to tell him the truth. If he did forgive her, she might be able to keep them together for a while longer yet.

But she still had no intention of ever telling him the entire truth of the past. That would hurt them both too much to bear.

Nor would she be saying anything anytime soon about how she had always loved him. She'd read and heard from other women that there was no surer way to lose a man than to hold commitment over his head. And Chase had already reacted badly to what he'd called her "invisible strings."

So she swore to keep her love a well-guarded secret.

Time. Kate needed a lot more time with him before they parted. And more time was all that mattered to her now.

A half hour later Chase got up from the table and moved in behind Kate at the sink. She was humming to herself and washing dishes at the same time.

Lost in her own world, she stared out the kitchen window at the spring sun beating down on the green lawns and gardens. The wild ebony curls that she'd tried to tame into a tight tail swayed back and forth as she swung her hips in time to whatever song was playing in her head. And for some reason the sight of that tail drove him crazy with lust.

The short white shorts she wore cupped her bottom and rode up her cheeks as she moved. From this close, he caught the scent of her, camellias and gardenia, the same as always. Those smells had haunted his life for twenty years. As a teenager, he'd thought them old-fashioned. Then as an adult, thinking of them at all made him angry, reminding him of betrayal and humiliation.

This morning those scents were giving him a savage hunger to take her right here—in the kitchen, despite the fact that they'd been making love pretty much constantly for the past twelve hours straight. His own stamina had surprised the hell out of him. But every time he looked at her…

He refused to give any serious consideration to the subject of just how much he wanted to make love with her again, however. It made her too important to his happiness—to his future. Kate was his history. He wanted a few weeks of her in his bed. After that, he intended for her to go right back into his past where she belonged.

But…there was lots of time yet. Time to enjoy being able to touch and to taste…to build her into a frenzy…then watch her explode just for him. Her face was so expressive, so full of life. He intended to be the cause of every emotion that filled those eyes and parted those full lips. It had become a kind of challenge.

Stepping directly behind her and sliding his arms around her waist, he dragged her up against his body. She sighed and leaned back against his chest.

Chase couldn't help himself, he bent his head and tasted the tender spot on her neck that he remembered drove her wild. She moaned and arched her back, giving his hands and mouth access to the places silently calling his name.

He inched his hands under her T-shirt, slid them up her rib cage and cupped her breasts. The tender weight of her in his palms spurred him on. He began rubbing her nipples right through the cotton bra, and thrilled to her moans in response. Furious heat rushed headlong to every inch of his body when she began to grind her hips back against the fullness that lay directly underneath his zipper.

He eyed the kitchen table and wondered if it was sturdy enough to hold them both, or if he should drag her to the floor with him instead. There wasn't much chance of them making it up the stairs to a bed.

Somewhere in the distance and through the lust clogging his brain, Chase thought he heard noises that hadn't been there a minute ago. One sound was like a truck's gears, grinding and straining close by.

Then another noise began penetrating through the thick sensual fog enveloping the two of them. He lifted his head and realized someone was pounding on the back door and calling Kate's name.

Dropping his hands and quickly stepping away, Chase tried to get himself under control as he strode slowly toward the kitchen door. He bit his tongue and surreptitiously adjusted his jeans. Close call.

When he opened the door, Shelby and Maddie smiled up at him. "Morning, Chase. There's a huge semitrailer coming up the allée. Tell Kate to come quick."

"Hell," he said under his breath. "I forgot." But by then, Shelby and the baby had bounded off the back steps and disappeared around the corner of the house.

"Forgot what?" Kate asked as she appeared beside him.

One look at her, with her flushed face and hardened nipples straining up toward him, and he dammed near forgot his own name.

But he sucked it up and shrugged one shoulder. "I ordered a few things."

"A few things? What kind of things?" She stuck her head out the door and stretched as though she could see around the solid walls to the front of the house.

"I guess I'd better go check off the bill of lading. Make sure it's all been delivered correctly."

She folded her arms across her chest, frowned up at him and tapped a toe with feigned impatience. "What things?" she demanded. All the while she was obviously trying to keep a straight face. She'd recognized that he'd been teasing, and was teasing him in return.

Her phoney frown made her look adorable and turned him on again. "Well, don't just stand there," he said instead of grabbing her up again. He had to move. "Let's go see." He had to get away from her heat.

Kate took a shortcut through the house and got there ahead of him. By the time he'd walked the distance around the house to the veranda, the delivery men were off-loading the first item. And the small audience that had gathered was all but holding its collective breath in anticipation.

"A brand-new John Deere," Shelby said as it came off the truck. "Wow. No more babying that old relic, Kate. Think of that."

"A new riding mower," Kate whispered reverently. She looked astonished.

Good. He'd hoped she would be surprised. It was all he'd been able to think about yesterday at the dealer. Surprising Kate and getting her to smile.

But she didn't smile. Not yet. At that moment one of the men began to unload the other items Chase had ordered. Kate dashed from box to box, checking out all his purchases.

Finally she turned to him. "Chase, what have you done? Why…?"

She looked like a kid who'd been given a surprise day off from school. Another expression he'd never seen on her face before.

He fisted his hands in his pockets to keep from reaching for her. "Now that I own this plantation, I want to protect my investment. It's past time for somebody to fix this old place up."

"Fix the place…" Kate spun around just as the ladders, paint and roofing supplies were being rolled down the truck's ramp.

She was stunned. Chase had bought the supplies necessary to fix up her family's home. Tears swam in her eyes, but she battled them back and reminded herself that the plantation no longer belonged to her family. Still, just being able to see the house and grounds brought back to their former glory would be a wonderful dream come true.

Kate turned to Chase, eager to ask about details. But the morning sun glared, making her shade her eyes.

"Who's going to do the work?" she asked with her hand against her forehead, blocking the light.

He shrugged. "I'd like to do some of it myself, but my time is limited. I'd thought…"

"Will you hire local contractors?" she interrupted. "There are tons of people without work in this parish."

"You really have so little faith in my ability to bring the mill back to profit?" he asked soberly. But she could swear she saw a twinkle spark in his eyes and little lines appear around his mouth.

Damn. The man was teasing her again. She'd always believed he didn't have a playful bone in his body, and yet here he was with a glint in his eyes and the edges of his lips ready to turn up in an out-and-out smirk.

And the strangest thing was…he had actually said he'd planned to try putting the mill back in business. Her heart skipped wildly, but she vowed to stay calm. She needed more information.

Except—she couldn't stop the wide smile that crept across her face. "No, of course not. But even if you can work a miracle for the mill, it will be months, maybe a year or two before everything can be up and running full force. In the meantime, couldn't you give a few people the chance to earn some money right here?"

Chase tilted his head and seemed to be seriously considering her question. Kate knew it was an act. He'd already made the decision and was still playing with her. But his new persona was intriguing. Who was this man?

"Well, yes," he answered at last. "I suppose that would be more efficient than importing help from the city. But I don't have a clue who around here is best to hire for this kind of work. By any chance do you know a general contractor I can get to oversee the job?"

"Let me handle it," she squeaked. Kate threw back her head and laughed. The first real laugh she'd managed in years.

He nodded and chuckled, with a more subtle match to her glee. "Just as long as you still have time to be my assistant at the mill…and can keep your evenings free."

The sensual look on his face shot a fiery spark bouncing through her chest and landing between her legs. It took her breath away. But she had to hold the desire down for now. Later they would have all night for her to show him her appreciation.

"Cool! You won't be sorry, Chase." She beamed at him and immediately started making lists in her head of things she needed to do.

He signed the invoice and handed it back to the driver. After fifteen minutes of checking off the delivery, Chase's body still hummed with lusty tension. And there didn't seem to be a single thing he could do to quell it.

Kate had actually laughed out loud. He searched his memory but couldn't think of a time when he'd seen her do that before. It was fascinating. Beguiling. Bewitching.

She had him twisted into hotter knots than he'd ever dreamed possible.

The truck driver made some comment from behind his back, but all Chase could think of was the heat. Kate was getting under his skin again. He'd sworn he wouldn't allow himself to be blindsided by her—not ever again.

Yet here he was, after only fifteen minutes of not being beside her, and already he felt desperate. His chest had begun to tighten with tension and desire. Where was she?

Looking around, he spotted her instantly. It was as though the sun had put her in a golden spotlight. She was standing in the middle of the lawn, while the sunshine sparkled off her raven hair. Heat shimmered up in waves from the still-wet grass, making everything seem to blur around the edges.

When Chase could focus past the glitter, he saw Kate with one hand on her hip. She was using the other hand to point out where the deliverymen should place the boxes and ladders.

Bathed in the sun's warm yellow glow, she appeared to be very much the spectacular and efficient dictator. He smiled at the idea.

But something about the sight of her didn't sit right. Kate had always been the *darkness* in his soul, not the *light*. And right at this moment she was the most brilliant, shining ray of light he'd ever seen—rare and dazzling.

Chase's hand automatically went to his shirt pocket.

He palmed the egg, letting its warmth and electricity soothe his nerves. The first strange thing he noticed after that was his chest muscles beginning to relax, maybe for the first time in months.

He kept his hand on the egg and watched as Shelby brought her baby over to Kate. After a second's discussion, the young mother placed Maddie in Kate's outstretched arms and headed back toward the house.

Kate shifted the toddler to her hip without missing a beat and continued with her directions to the men. The baby looked up with wonder, staring at the animated face of the woman who held her.

Chase knew exactly how the kid was feeling. Kate seemed different all of a sudden. Competent, strong and so damned sexy his mouth watered. She simply amazed him.

Absently rubbing the egg in his pocket again for comfort, Chase realized he was suddenly changed, too. Something inside him was breaking down, crumbling. And he couldn't quite get a handle on what it was—or how to stop it.

The rest of Sunday afternoon went by in a blur for Kate.

Shelby spent the day in the kitchen, preparing a meal she'd been hired to cater for a party of forty. So Kate and Maddie and Chase had strolled the grounds of Live Oak Hall, dreaming of how the place would look after restoration.

She and Chase had a few heated discussions as they strolled. "I like the house painted that natural green color. It's been that way as long as I can remember," she'd argued.

But Chase won her over to his side of the paint debate by having done his homework. He'd discovered that flat ivory was the original house color. And he insisted nothing else would do except that the plantation be refurbished to look the same as it had when first built.

Impressed, Kate readily gave in.

Later they sat in the kitchen as Shelby fed them a few of the selections she would be serving at the party. Jambalaya, barbecued shrimp, rum-laced bread pudding. Partly it was a taste test, but mostly Shell had simply wanted company while she cooked.

Chase asked a load of questions about her catering business while they ate. Shelby rattled on and on with him companionably. The whole scene seemed amazingly cozy and friendly. Something Kate had experienced little of in her lifetime.

When Shell changed the topic of conversation to painters and carpenters, Kate gladly made copious mental notes about the workers her friend discussed. Kate wanted to be ready tomorrow to take bids.

The only thing that tripped Kate up during the whole wonderful afternoon was the sight of Chase, feeding Maddie and then rocking the sleepy toddler to sleep in his arms for her nap. He'd done it easily, even casually, as the grown-ups had continued with their conversations.

"What are you doing?" she'd asked him as he spooned a bite into the baby's waiting mouth.

He shrugged absently, but kept right on as if he did such things every day.

Busy Shelby paid little attention to what he was doing, but then the baby's mother didn't know Chase all that well, either. Maybe she thought such behavior was natural for him.

Kate, on the other hand, had been stunned into silence. The sight of the town's bad boy gently attending to a baby took her by surprise. Had he really changed so much? First the house refurbishment, now fatherly tenderness?

Later, after Shelby packed up both Maddie and the food and left for her job, Chase suggested the two of them sit on the veranda to watch the sun set. Another out of character suggestion from him, Kate went along with it but began to worry that this was all some kind of act.

They sat in the rockers, silently watching as the shadows grew longer across the lawn. Her mind began racing again.

Was he deliberately leading her along? Lulling her into believing he'd changed and fooling her into falling even deeper in love with him?

Could this new persona possibly be his own diabolical method of exacting revenge? Perhaps making the house a gorgeous showplace and then kicking her out to drool over it from afar was his goal.

But that answer didn't feel right. If that's what he was doing, he had certainly carried the whole thing too far.

Besides, making her love him more was not a possibility. She was already in deep. And losing the house would be nothing compared to losing him.

As the setting sun shot dazzling rays of orange and lavender over the bayou, Kate quietly shook her head and vowed not to ask. It was a hopeless situation.

And she was already utterly—hopelessly—lost in love.

# Nine

"**I** give up," Chase complained after yet another frustrating morning. "We're moving into the conference room with the computer so we can set up flow charts. Get Rose and all the files you think might help explain these figures and then meet me there."

Kate shook herself free of the sensual dreams that captured her attention whenever Chase was near, and left his office to do as he'd asked. What an odd ten days they'd just lived through. Both good and bad, the time she'd spent with him had left her alternately confused and dazzled.

If she'd thought that first dreamy, Cinderella Sunday afternoon had been a big blur, then all the nights in the past ten days had proven just how really blurry life with Chase could become.

Each night they spent long hours filled with soft,

sensual cries, hardened bodies and silky mind-bending temptations. It had seemed like a passion-filled miracle.

But as each dawn broke to reveal melancholy light-gray drizzle, the magic disappeared. Rainy mornings foreshadowed the nasty reality of frustrating days. Days spent searching for salvation for the mill. Ten endless days filled with damp raincoats and soggy shoes.

Later that same afternoon, long after they'd moved to the conference room, Chase pushed back his chair and frowned. "It's dark. You look tired, *chère*. Shall we call it a day?"

Rose had left for home an hour ago. Evening shadows had begun to trace spooky designs over a conference table stacked high with files. And darkness was falling eerily across the computer screen, where dire cost figures blinked out a hideous green pattern.

"I'm fine. Just annoyed that there doesn't seem to be any good answers for the mill," Kate told him as she rubbed a hand over her eyes.

She didn't look fine to Chase. Tiny lines etched her forehead, and faint purple smudges appeared under her eyes.

He drove a hand through his hair and wished for the hundredth time that they had never started this fruitless quest. The weary look on Kate's face tonight was not one he would ever have chosen for her.

"You know, it almost seems as if your father deliberately ran the mill into the ground," Chase offered. "I thought he was just incompetent, but this…"

Kate laid a hand on his sleeve in a patient gesture. "For as long as I can remember, my father hated everything and everyone. His parents. My mother. This town. It's entirely possible that he hated the mill and all that it represented, too."

"If he hated the place so much, why stick around?" Chase asked. "When *his* father died, he could've sold the business off at a profit and lived on the proceeds."

"I think…" Kate hesitated a second then folded her arms under her breasts. "Well, in my opinion, my father stayed here to exact a kind of revenge against my grandfather."

"But your grandfather died twelve years ago."

She nodded. "My grandfather deeply loved the business that generations of his family had cherished before him. He'd built the mill into an efficient showplace by the time he died. But he never did let his son have any part in running it.

"I'm not sure," she continued dryly. "But I don't think my grandfather ever truly believed my father was capable of becoming a manager. Unfortunately, when Grandfather died of a sudden heart attack, my father inherited the whole works…ready or not."

As she turned to look out the window at the black night, Kate's shoulders slumped with fatigue. "I'm pretty sure my father decided to manage the mill all by himself just to prove he could do it. But when things got tough, he refused to let go and hire someone better able to take over. By then the hate had eaten him away exactly like the cancer that eventually killed him."

It occurred to Chase that Kate had done almost the same thing when she stayed on to work at the mill. Her father had also refused to let *her* have a hand in running things—just the way her grandfather had treated him. Was her heart full of hate the way her father's had been?

Chase answered his own question with a resounding no. He'd seen no signs of hate from her since he'd been back in town. But perhaps it *had* been a kind of hatred that had caused Kate to tell the sheriff that story ten years ago. There had to be some reason why she'd lied.

"Do you have any ideas about where we should go from here?" he asked as he stood and rubbed his neck. Chase absolutely refused to dwell on the past for now. Not when the future for the mill looked so bleak. "Can you think of any avenue we haven't tried?"

Kate turned to him with a glimmer of hope in her eyes. "There is a possibility. I'd be willing to bet one or two of the rice farmers that used to do business with my grandfather could shed some light on where things went so wrong. Maybe they'd be able to give us some advice, too."

"That might not be such a bad idea." Remembering something he'd seen earlier, Chase picked up a folder, flipped it open and pointed out the reference. "These two farmers in the next parish actually still hold small liens against the company. They must've once thought the mill had a chance of recovery if they were willing to loan your father money."

She gazed up at him, and she looked so vulnerable…so needy. He couldn't seem to help himself. Pulling her to him, he wrapped Kate up in a protective embrace. She took a deep breath, as though she was afraid to be seen as weak. But then she collapsed against him, molded herself into his arms and hung on.

Knowing how much this ghost of a mill meant to her, Chase had worked hard, desperately trying to find a miracle that would save the place. Unfortunately, he was practically convinced now that nothing could ever bring it back. But as long as Kate still had that hope in her eyes, he wasn't willing to give up and tear the mill down—not yet.

He leaned his cheek on the top of her head and breathed in the familiar scent of her hair. The smell and texture turned him on—the same as every other time he'd held her in his arms.

"Maybe tomorrow we'll get a break in the weather," he offered. But his real thoughts were about later tonight when he could get her back into his bed. "If it clears off, let's try to get appointments to see those two farmers. Okay?"

She nodded quietly, snuggled up tighter under his chin and clung to him.

Wanting more than anything to tell her things would work out fine and that they would discover a secret to save the mill, Chase kept his mouth shut instead. He didn't want to give her false promises, so he stayed silent and held her.

Just held her.

"Well, look at you, Missy Katherine. A grown-up woman." Augustine St. Germaine, a seventy-year-old farmer and a longtime friend of her grandfather's, took her hand with an appreciative smile. "And a mighty fine-looking one, at that."

Kate felt the twinge of color move up her neck, but ignored it and leaned in to give him a peck on the cheek. "Thank you for seeing us, Gus. You are too kind. I want you to meet the new mill owner, Chase Severin."

"Severin? You must be Charles's son." The old man clapped Chase on the shoulder and beamed at him. "My great-grandfather brought the first Severin down to this corner of Louisiana. Hired him to manage the St. Germaine Plantation. Must've been your ancestor. Bet you didn't know that, did you?"

Chase shook his head once politely. "I'm the last Severin I know of to live in Louisiana, sir. My father lives in Houston now." He reached a hand out to shake the one Gus offered. "I really appreciate you giving up your time for Kate and me."

Gus nodded then tipped his chin. "Odd to think of a Severin owning the rice mill instead of a Beltrane. But then, at my age I've discovered there's plenty of unexplainable surprises in one's lifetime." He turned his head to look at Kate again. "And here a Beltrane's involved now, too. Isn't that right?"

He ushered them out to the table and chairs set up on his terrace. "The doctors only allow me iced tea these days. But I'd be pleased to scare up a bloody Mary or have a batch of julep mixed if that'd suit y'all better."

Kate smiled. Older…grayer…than she remembered, Gus St. Germaine was still every bit the Southern gentleman.

"No thank you, Gus. Chase found a notation about the mill still carrying an outstanding debt to you. We've…"

"Nonsense, Kate." Gus politely held her chair and they all sat down around the table. "I wrote that account off years ago. I'd always thought of it as a gift in your grandfather's memory, not like a true bad debt."

Chase acknowledged the generosity, then outlined

the reason they'd come. "Do you know of anything that we could try that might help us bring the mill back to its former glory? For instance, can you tell us why you don't have your rice milled there anymore?"

Kate poured the iced teas, making sure Gus's was just as he liked it. And then she nodded, encouraging the old man to speak plainly.

Gus sat back and sipped his tea thoughtfully. "My time is almost done, son. I have a granddaughter who manages the St. Germaine Plantation's farming operations these days. She's brought us right into the twenty-first century."

Gus smiled wryly. "Sometimes kicking, screaming and dragging our heels, mind you. But there you go. We don't even grow rice anymore. Not profitable enough now, she claims."

"Your granddaughter manages the entire operation?" Kate was stunned. She'd never heard of a woman plantation manager before.

"Sure enough," Gus told her. "That one's smarter than all the rest of us by a mile. You remind me of her some, Missy Katherine. Full of that womanly Southern charm you were born to. But by the same token, you strike me as one female who stays ten jumps ahead of every man around you."

Kate murmured a thank-you. But instead of the feminine blush expected of a Southern lady, she lifted her chin and glanced over at Chase. She wondered what he thought of her capabilities, but imagined that she would never know for sure. The black day when he would be leaving the parish—and her—behind seemed to be getting closer every minute.

"Are all the farmers around here switching their crops and not planting rice?" Chase asked.

"I'd say so," Gus allowed. "Those that haven't sold off farms to oil companies or land developers, that is. Gotta keep up with the times. St. Germaine's farm even got us a computer system that decides what to plant and when to harvest. Damnedest thing."

There wasn't much left that Gus could tell them, so they finished their tea and bid him goodbye. Their next stop turned out to be just as depressing. That old rice grower had sold off all his land several years back and now was enjoying a wealthy retirement sitting on his veranda.

Back in Chase's convertible on the way home, Kate wasn't sure what to say. "It certainly looks hopeless for the mill, doesn't it?"

"I'm sorry, *chère*. I don't see any way out of it." Chase shook his head sadly. "Even if your father hadn't mismanaged the mill, it's in a dying industry. Eventually everything would've come to the same result. Are you horribly disappointed that your family's heritage can't be resurrected?"

The sun shone brightly on their bare heads, highlighting the chestnut streaks in his hair. He flipped his sunglasses out of the glove box and slid them in place.

Chase looked so handsome, she thought as they raced along the country blacktop in his Jaguar with the top down. Dressed in a pair of black jeans, a charcoal-gray T-shirt, and with a saddle-colored suede jacket slung over the backseat, he reminded Kate of every erotic notion she'd ever had.

She had been touched to hear Chase actually say he was

sorry for the loss of her family's dream. And though empathy wouldn't save the town, his tenderness amazed her.

Her heart twitched and had her wishing she could reach for him right here. Instead she clasped her hands in her lap. Tonight couldn't come soon enough.

"I'm not disappointed about the mill." She decided to tell him the truth, trying to make things easier between them. "It was never the actual mill that I cared about. I just wanted to give all the employees their old jobs back. It's the town and the people I was desperate to keep alive, not that broken-down old mill."

Chase slanted a glance in her direction, and for a second his expression turned quizzical. He studied her. Kate wasn't exactly sure what she'd said that bothered him, but in a few moments he turned back to concentrate on the road ahead.

She was grateful the discussion of the mill had stopped, though. It was too nice a day for that.

A minute later he raised a wicked eyebrow and asked, "You ready for that picnic lunch Shelby packed for us, *chère?* I have someplace special in mind where we can be alone, if you think you're ready to eat."

Kate was starving. Starving for a few last hours alone with the love of her life.

"I'm hungry," she said with a wide smile. "And more than ready."

Chase turned down the old country lane that headed off through Blackwater Bayou toward the river. He heard Kate gulp in a breath and knew she'd finally figured out where they were headed. He would've thought she'd known the minute he had said it was a special place.

He'd liked the way Kate had started out the day, all neat and tidy in light gray slacks and silky silver blouse. Her hair had been tied up and the soft black curls tamed. She'd appeared to be every bit the businesswoman as they'd made their calls to the plantation owners.

Now the wind had stirred more than a few of her curls out of their bounds, the sun was pinking her nose and the tails of the blouse hung loose to her hips. He'd decided he liked the vision she made this way a lot better. It was much more Kate than Katherine.

"We're so *not* going to that old willow," she said as her jaw tensed and her shoulders tightened. "It's going to be all muddy from days of rain. Besides, you really don't want to bring up all those bad memories, do you?"

"You think there will be ghosts in our old place, *chère?* Perhaps we need to exorcise them. Cast them out with the other devils from our past."

Chase was beginning to feel rather tense himself. But he'd dreamed of this place and this woman for ten long years, and today they would close the book on that miserable chapter in their lives. Start again fresh.

Her father was gone. The mill was about to become just a memory. Everything was different for them these days.

He needed the closure. There would be no leaving town again until they'd come full circle.

Kate leaned back and closed her eyes to the harsh sun. It wasn't that she didn't want him. It wasn't even that she minded making love to him in the middle of the day and outside under their old tree. She didn't.

What troubled her was having to face her guilt head-on. If they made love in their old place today, she knew the truth would come out.

She'd almost told him a dozen times over the past two weeks, but held the words in, knowing it would probably mean the end for them. Now that the future of the mill was no longer in question and the construction workers would begin restorations on Live Oak Hall tomorrow, her time with Chase had clearly narrowed down to a few more days at most.

Wiping away the lone tear leaking from the corner of her eye, Kate swallowed back the pain and decided to make the most of their last few hours. She owed him that much.

First they would have their picnic. Then they would lose themselves in each other's arms, just the way she imagined he'd been dreaming about for all these long years. And finally she would give him his answers.

For she too had dreamed. Dreamed of going back to change everything. And, today was that day. The end of dreams.

"Look, Kate. Our willow is sitting high and dry. The course of the river must've changed over the past ten years." Chase pulled the car to a stop a few yards away, jumped out and headed for the trunk and the picnic supplies.

As he stuffed the car keys back into his pocket, he spent just a second running his fingers over the smooth surface of his lucky egg. Wondering if the river's change of course was a good omen, he figured maybe he and Kate were about to have a change in the course of their lives as well.

Being here might be as difficult for him as it was for her. But they needed a new beginning, and what better place to start again?

\* \* \*

Deep in the shadows of Blackwater Bayou, the old gypsy woman nodded her head and cackled. "You have no idea how much the course of your lives is about to change, young Severin." *Lucky* egg—indeed.

Gypsy magic took no luck. It took only skill and true belief.

Everything was in place and ready. She slipped the crystal into her pocket and rubbed her hands together. It wouldn't be long now.

Surely she had made the best preparations possible. This young Steele heir would shortly be forced to accept his inheritance. The true magic would make all the difference.

Promises would finally be kept and secrets would be revealed.

Kate lay back on her elbows and watched as Chase peeled an orange. She was feeling languid and lazy and fat as a tick. The poorboy sandwiches had been terrific and as usual they were more than filling. Shelby was really clever to pack fruit for dessert instead of loading up the basket with a heavier sweet after all that food.

Waiting for Chase to take the first bite, she was surprised when he held a slice to her lips. "You first, *chère.*"

There was no mistaking the look in his eyes. His hunger had certainly not been sated by food. The heat in those deep-gray eyes made it clear what he wanted next. And it wasn't an orange.

He slipped the slice into her mouth. She took it along

with the tips of his fingers. Savoring both, the citrusy taste along with the erotic touch of skin caused explosions on her tongue. Sweet and absolutely perfect, she couldn't help the small moan of pleasure as juice escaped her lips and dribbled down her chin.

Chase's eyes narrowed…darkened. He pulled his fingers free just as she'd swiped a hand across her chin to contain the juice.

He captured that hand and ever so slowly licked each finger. When he ended by drawing circles with the tip of his tongue across her palm, Kate began to pant.

Picking up another juicy orange slice, Chase took it into his mouth, then leaned in to slant a kiss across her lips. A riot of flavors and sticky sweet juices turned the plain orange into a sinful treasure shared in their mouths.

She mumbled words of shock and disbelief against his lips, letting the juice roll down her neck and flow between her breasts. Kate could swear there was a steamy orange juice mist rising between them.

There would be no help for Chase's frantic craving to have this woman beneath him. Neither of them were exactly the same people as they had been ten years ago. But he'd ached to have her here under their tree again for all that time. Why fight it?

Leaning over her, he possessively molded her breasts with his hands. Her body began to vibrate under him, sending sizzling currents through them both.

Sweet and sticky, he nibbled his way down her neck at the same time he used one hand to unbutton her shirt. "You are so…" No words could describe what he was feeling at the moment. Every image, every adjective was inadequate and paled in comparison to the reality of Kate.

She melted into him, going soft and fluid just as he went hard. Their need was suddenly insane and rash.

He tried to hold on to sanity, but found that nearly impossible to accomplish. They began tearing wildly at each other's clothing. One last fleeting rational thought reminded him of the foil packets he'd put into his pocket in anticipation of being here with her.

So as he scrambled out of his slacks he dug one up, tore it open and covered himself. He stopped then, for just a moment, hovering over her and savoring the sight of her lying naked looking up at him. It was his dream.

Her eyes were glazed with passion as she reached out to run her hands across his chest. A flash of memory clogged his throat, and the wistful sting of remembered desire clouded his eyes.

Kate arched up to him and nipped at his nipples, using her teeth and tongue to push him on. The pleasure verged on pain, jumbling in his mind.

He bent to her, teasing, tasting, driving them both upward on a fast hot ride.

Kate gasped, ran her fingers through his hair and held him in place. She dug her nails into his back as she arched her hips.

"Chase," she whispered. "This…this is so different. I feel…so different."

He managed a smile as he held himself slightly above her. "Different good? Or different bad?"

"I don't know," she said on a low moan. "It's just more. I'm desperate…frantic…to feel you inside of me. If I don't have you there soon, I think I might die."

"My sentiments exactly, *chère*."

Giving in to his body's command, he pushed inside

her on one long, slow, exquisite glide. Chase closed his eyes and experienced the velvet feel of her body surrounding him, wrapping around him like a sensual vice grip.

His mind blanked as he heard the word "more" repeating in his ears. She was *more*. Together they became *more*. *More* than just one.

Rocking his body into hers, the blood rushing through his veins, he pulled her with him as he urged her to climb higher. He thrust and she met him, time and again.

Too soon he felt her internal muscles sucking him deeper into her body and releasing the flood of dizzying stars that would quickly capture them both.

Kate screamed his name. His voice broke on hers. They collapsed in a heap, holding each other as the pleasurable ripples subsided.

When the blood stopped rushing in his ears, he rolled to one side and spat out a curse.

She sat up, gasping for a ragged breath. "What's the matter?"

Chase sat up, too, and rubbed a hand over his eyes. "Please tell me it doesn't matter that the condom just broke."

"I…" She reached for her blouse. "You're kidding, right?"

"Wish I was. We need to figure out how bad this might be. Where are you in your cycle?"

Shoving her arms through the sleeves of her blouse, Kate tried to calm down and think. But the math betrayed her. This simply could not be happening. Had she learned nothing at all from her past?

"I'm four days late."

"Oh, God."

She blinked her eyes and decided it was time to panic. Scrambling to get dressed and using his own words, she mimicked, "My sentiments exactly."

Chase paced down the hallway right outside the bathroom. "How long has it been now?"

"Time will not go any faster if you ask that same question every ten seconds." She glared at him.

He glared back, shrugged and paced the hall.

Kate hugged herself around the waist but refused to stare down at the pregnancy test wand sitting on the counter. She stormed down the hall in the opposite direction.

This was too much a repeat of the past. She couldn't face it. She'd been lying to herself and wasn't strong enough. She hadn't even had a chance to tell him what had really happened the night he left town.

Guilt, panic, hysteria…they all combined to drive Kate over an edge. "You might've at least gone out and bought a new box of the damned things," she snapped. "Just because it was a fifty-pack, you didn't have to rely solely on me for our supply."

Chase turned and paced toward her. "Are you implying that a twenty-year-old box of expired condoms might not be totally reliable? What a shock."

"And that would be all my fault…how?"

"Dammit, Kate," he said with a grimace. "Maybe you're late due to stress or something. Just because one condom in the box was bad doesn't mean they all were."

"Hey. Wishful thinking is always such a big help in a crisis. That'll make everything *so* much bet.…"

"How long has it been now?" he interrupted.

She checked the wall clock. "Three minutes. It's probably ready." But her feet refused to move.

Chase hesitated, looked at her for a second, then walked into the bathroom and picked up the wand. "We'll both look at the same time, okay?"

Her heart moved into her throat. "Right. On three. One…two…"

# Ten

"**W**e'll get married."

Kate shoved at Chase's chest, then fisted her hands. "Don't be ridiculous."

"Why is that ridiculous? When people make babies together, they get married."

Since the moment they'd both seen the plus sign, Kate's mind had been racing. Right along with her heart.

She folded her arms across her chest with a grimace. "But not us. You said you wanted things to be temporary. Why would you marry me?"

He took a step toward her, then hesitated, as though changing his mind. "I'd have thought my feelings would be rather easy to guess after the last couple of weeks."

Not so much, she thought wryly. There had been times when she'd imagined that he really cared for her.

But then, in the next instant, everything would dissolve into a lust-filled haze, blurring whatever other feelings might exist between them.

She knew he wanted her—craved her—exactly the way she craved him. But what else was there to fall back on? Nothing but distrust.

That had been the real reason she had not told him the truth of their past yet. She loved the fact that he still desired her body. And she hadn't wanted to see the end of their time together come too soon. It was selfish, sure. But there it was.

"Okay," she agreed. "So we have great sex…um… more than great. But that's not a good enough reason for two people to marry."

Chase's expression turned down in a scowl. "Just sex?" This time he moved quickly and placed both hands on her shoulders to keep her from backing away. "That's what you think we…?"

Without finishing the thought, he silently scanned her face, looking for some basic truth he must've wanted to see. Kate tried to block the emotions from shining through in her eyes. She couldn't bear for him to know everything. It would make her too vulnerable.

She pulled her shoulder free from his grasp. "Look, Chase, let's think about this rationally. You have businesses that need you to go to far-flung places. Pretty soon the mill will be gone and you'll have no reason to stay here in Bayou City at all.

"I on the other hand have no reason to leave," she continued. "This is my home. I can raise my child here with the help of my friends."

"Then you do intend to have this child?"

"What?" The question was such a shock, Kate had to take a moment to breathe. "Yes, of course I do."

Chase's eyes were nearly black with emotions Kate couldn't begin to imagine. "And you intend to be a single mother in a town that has no industry and no means to earn a living?"

"I can find some way to support myself and my child. Look at Shelby. She's doing okay."

"Perhaps…with your help. But Maddie is not my child." He closed the gap she'd put between them. "Shelby had no choice in the matter. I do. My child will not grow up never knowing its father."

*Too close,* she thought. When he's too close, I can't think.

She turned again and walked to the head of the main staircase. "I'm trying to be reasonable here, Chase. If you want to participate in your child's life…even give us financial support…I won't stop you."

Kate started down the stairs, addressing him over her shoulder. "But that's no reason for you to give up your freedom and tie yourself down with a woman you don't trust and will never love."

He reached her on the landing. "Stop it, Kate." Swinging her around, Chase pulled her close. "You're running again. Why?"

Kate bit down on her panic and tried to relax her shoulders. The time for running was over at last.

"All right, Chase." She took him by the hand. "Come with me to the kitchen. I have something to tell you."

Chase had mixed feelings about what Kate would say. He had wondered about that night for ten miserable years. He'd made up every excuse in the book for her behavior, and now he wasn't sure he wanted to know the truth.

It would change everything.

He needed a cigar to get through her story. No. He needed a good stiff shot of bourbon. No, not that either.

After pouring Kate a glass of water and himself a cup of chicory coffee, he palmed his lucky egg and immediately felt stronger. "Sit down, *chère*. I want to hear everything right from the beginning."

She was trembling slightly, and her vulnerability made his heart flip wildly in his chest. "Are you cold? Do you need a sweater?"

Kate shook her head and slumped into one of the kitchen chairs. "Thanks, no. I just need to find the words."

He pulled out his own chair and joined her. "That should be fairly easy. Just start with the *why*."

Blinded by the sincere expression on his face, Kate tried to shake the picture in her head of Chase as a teenager. He had been so handsome and exciting…the town's bad boy who was secretly just a lost and lonely kid. And she'd been the lonely little girl who had secretly loved him. They'd become friends. Then they had become lovers.

That was the real beginning to their story.

But that wasn't where she wanted to start. She didn't want to begin from the moment they'd first made love—or the time he first told her that he loved her, either.

Instead she began with the end. "Before I sneaked out to meet you that last night, my father and I had a terrible fight. He'd…well somehow he'd found out we had been seeing each other. And he knew…he knew how close we'd become."

A sharp look of confusion filled Chase's eyes. She couldn't allow him to ask any questions, questions that might come too close to all of the truth. So she hurriedly continued with her story.

"I made the mistake of telling him that we planned on running away together. I know it wasn't the truth, but I had to make him stop threatening to cut me off. It was all I could think of, letting him believe we could take care of ourselves and didn't need him or his money."

"Why didn't you tell me?"

"Because it wasn't true," she sighed. "I didn't really believe I could get along without his money. I was young, Chase. Seventeen. You didn't have a real job. I was scared."

"And spoiled," he added softly.

"Yes, all right. And spoiled." She hadn't remained spoiled for long. Kate had grown up fast. But she wasn't ready to let go of all her secrets.

"I imagined that I could just stay out of the house for one night and then go back the next day and he'd be so glad to see me everything would be okay again." She took a sip of water, but noticed her hand was shaking, so she set the glass back down. "I hadn't counted on the extent of my father's hatred of both you and your father. I didn't know he'd stop at nothing to keep me from leaving town with you."

Guilt had been her constant companion for ten years. It was hard now, admitting her mistakes. Hard to watch Chase's face as he heard the truth.

"But you didn't know your father set me up? That he had hired those boys to run me out of town."

"No, of course I didn't know. I wouldn't have…" She let the words trail off. It was too late to claim total innocence. "I was just as surprised as you were when Justin-Roy and those boys showed up."

Chase's face filled with confusion and hurt. "Then why, Kate? Why did you lie to the sheriff?"

She wanted to scream her excuses at him once more. She had been young. She had been scared. But they all sounded so hollow.

"The sheriff called my father when we first got to the station and made me talk to him on the phone," she admitted. "Father said I had to agree with the boys' account of what happened or else… Or else he would press charges against you for statutory rape. He told me he could make it stick no matter what I said, and that you would be sent to prison for twenty years hard labor."

"What?" Chase's face was a mask, so she rushed on.

"I couldn't let that happen. Don't you see? It was all my fault. I couldn't bear to have you put in prison because of my family. It would've killed me."

A new look that just appeared on his face told her everything. It said if he could strangle her right now, it would be too quick and easy. It was difficult to see him this angry. But it wasn't any worse than she had expected.

Chase pushed back his chair and stood. "Why didn't you tell me this that night? Why didn't you try to find me to tell me later?"

"I didn't have a chance that night. My father came and dragged me home. But I did try to find you…later. You seemed to have disappeared off the face of the earth." She wasn't prepared to go into that part of the story, however.

Looking off into space as if he'd been struck dumb, Chase appeared blindsided…as though his mind refused to take it all in.

"Can I do anything? Get you anything?" She was starting to worry about him. This had to have been a huge shock.

He shook his head. "I need a little time."

"What does that mean? Are you leaving?"

"I'll contact you tomorrow," he said as he turned and stormed through the house to the front door.

When she heard his car start up and then listened while the engine noises receded into the night, Kate's nerves finally gave up. She crumbled back into her chair in a sorry heap and cried the tears that she'd thought had dried up years ago.

Madder than hell, Chase downshifted the Jag and took the river road curve at sixty.

Frustrated. Stunned. But most of all furious, Chase beat his fists against the steering wheel.

He could not take revenge against a frigging ghost. Dammit! And it was the ghost of Henry Beltrane that he now knew for sure deserved all his anger.

Unbelievable. The bastard had actually used his young, scared seventeen-year-old daughter and forced her to lie for him. If Chase knew where the devil's grave was, he might be tempted to dig him up and kill him—again.

Every time from now on that Chase thought of how undeservedly guilty Kate had been for the last ten years—and of how he himself had wrongly thought it was her that should be punished for betraying him—

*"Et là!"* he swore, as he put his foot on the gas pedal and roared down the country roads.

Dark questions still swirled in the back of his mind. Why had Kate's father hated the Severin family badly enough to force Chase out of town? And who had told Henry Beltrane that his daughter and Chase had been intimate? No one else should've known that.

He'd thought when Kate explained about that last night, he would have all the answers. But he only had more questions.

Hell! All this anger swirling inside his heart and no way to take revenge.

For several hours Chase drove down deserted lanes. He had to find some plan for getting even with a ghost.

In a way, it was a good thing Beltrane was already dead.

Chase slowed the car at a stop sign. Instead of revenge, his mind kept focusing on how blessed he and Kate were to be having a child on the way. A brand-new generation of Severins soon living in St. Mary's parish.

Raking his fingers through his hair in frustration, Chase tried to devise a plan of how to make his child's life better than his had been. And at the same time exact a measure of revenge against the ghost who haunted him.

An idea began to percolate in the back of Chase's mind. He turned the car around and headed toward Highway 90 that would take him into New Orleans.

Just maybe there *was* a way....

The sun had driven the gray shadows of dawn back into the swamp before Kate finally dragged herself out of bed and made it down to the kitchen for coffee. She hadn't slept and couldn't manage to stop the tears long enough to take a shower or get dressed.

Chase had left all his things when he turned his back and walked out of her life last night. Would she ever see him again? Or would he simply call and tell her where to forward his stuff?

For a few shining minutes when they'd first found out she was pregnant, Kate had really started to hope. But she'd always known the day of reckoning was coming. The day when the truth of that awful night would come out.

And now it had. But it was really only fair that Chase knew the truth.

Kate sighed. There was more. More that Chase probably should know.

But she couldn't make herself tell him about that. She had never told anyone but her father. Ever.

And now… A chill ran up her arms, raising the tiny hairs and bringing goose bumps.

Now that she was pregnant, she couldn't even bear to think of it herself, let alone speak the words. She combed a hand through her hair, leaned against the kitchen counter for support and tried to banish the memory for good.

Without Chase in her life, nothing made much difference anyway.

"Morning, *chère*."

"Chase?" She spun at the sound of his voice. "Oh, thank heaven. Are you all right?"

He walked toward her but stopped just out of reach. "I'm okay. But you don't look as if you feel too well. Has it something to do with the pregnancy? Should you see a doctor?"

Her shoulders slumped and she swiped at her eyes. "No. I mean, I feel fine. Just tired. I was worried about you."

He grinned. "Well, except for a speeding ticket, I'm all in one piece." He raised a hand as though he wanted to touch her face, but too quickly he let it fall back into place.

"A ticket? But…"

Chase waved off the question. "I'm going upstairs to pack a bag. I have a plane to catch and not much time."

"Oh." The tiny hope that had almost sprung to life in her chest disappeared in a flash. "Can I help? Would you like breakfast?"

"Wish I had the time…for that and other things as well. But no, thanks."

"Uh, do you know when you'll be coming back?" It was a presumptive question. If she just assumed he would be coming home, then maybe it would be true.

"No," he said with a little hesitation in his voice. "I'm not sure. I hope it won't be too long."

Ah. There went that little ray of hope again.

She took a big leap of faith and decided to try pinning him down. "But then why are you going?"

"I have casino business to attend to. But I don't have any idea how long it will take."

Oh, well. That wasn't so bad. He was going on business. At least, she hoped he wasn't making it up for her benefit. Lots of men panicked when they first found out they were becoming fathers. And Chase had more reason to be wary of the child's mother than most.

"I want you to shut down the mill for good while I'm gone, *chère*."

Her heart sank. It was the end of an era and probably spelled doom for the town. But she'd known it was time.

"Box up the files and sell off as much of the office and mill equipment as you can," he continued. "Then I need you to be here to supervise the restoration crews."

"But…what about Rose?" Her secretary was the last mill employee besides herself. What would she do?

"Rose?" he asked thoughtfully. "Oh. Rose. She should still be your secretary for a while. You'll need help in closing down the mill, and then she can set up the payroll and files for the construction crews."

"So, it's okay if I stay here until the house construction is done?"

"Of course," he said with surprise. "This is your home for at least nine more months. I don't want you to have to move until after the baby comes."

All Kate heard of his comment was that after the baby came she would not be welcome to live in his house. The tears swam in her eyes again, but she held them back.

"All right, Chase. If that's what you want." She would not give him the satisfaction of seeing her misery.

"Great," he said as he turned to head up the stairs.

He stopped at the doorway and turned back to her. "We have lots to talk about, Kate. I had a fantastic…" He hesitated again. "There's no time now. We'll do this when I get back."

She looked up at the man she had loved for her whole life and managed a half smile. She had to hide her real desolation.

But when she smiled, his eyes lit up. He closed the gap between them with one step.

"Ah, *chère*, don't tempt me." He pulled her into his

arms and lasered a desperate kiss across her lips. "I have to go," he said when he raised his head at last.

"Will you be all right while I'm gone?" He kept her close to his body, and Kate felt his heart strumming wildly in his chest.

She nodded. "I'll be fine."

"Terrific." He ground his lips against hers again and groaned as he forced himself to let go and back away.

This time he made it all the way out the kitchen door before he turned around once more. "I almost forgot. While I'm gone, plan the wedding. Do it up however you want."

"Wedding? Us? But…"

"No buts, Kate. We're getting married. My child will carry my name and will start to feel my love before he's even born. It's a done deal." With that he dashed out of the kitchen and up the stairs.

Chase was still driving her crazy. What did he really feel for her? Was he mad or not?

Shaking her head, Kate decided she would just have to take it one step at a time.

For however long they had remaining.

# Eleven

Chase carefully guided the Jag through the deep twilight, as he drove down the allée drive toward Live Oak Hall. In the three weeks that he'd been gone, lots of changes had taken place at the plantation.

Construction equipment was spread out across the lawn, scaffolding had been erected against the walls of the house, and the old peeling green paint had been replaced by a rough-sanded look that was even worse. But Chase wasn't the least unhappy about the plantation's condition. It was progress. Progress toward a phenomenal ending.

He couldn't wait to see Kate. To tell her that he'd done it. Actually done it. As far-fetched as it had sounded at first, the wheels were in motion that would make his plan come true.

Barely containing his excitement, Chase found a spot

to park that looked safe enough under a tall crepe myrtle tree. He wanted to see Kate for another reason, too. He'd only managed a handful of calls while he'd been out of town. Twice he had actually reached Shelby instead of Kate. Now he needed to see Kate, to hear her voice, to touch her.

On the drive down from Baton Rouge, it had belatedly hit him that not only hadn't he told Kate his plan, but he also hadn't told her he loved her. Not getting her hopes up by sharing the details of a risky plan was one thing. But not telling the woman you intended to marry that you loved her was sheer lunacy.

A mistake he intended to rectify immediately.

He bounded out of the car by vaulting over the door instead of opening it. Heading for the kitchen where lights were blazing, Chase palmed the lucky egg that he now kept with him at all times.

It had truly been a blessed day when that old gypsy had gifted him with this legacy. Safe and secure in his world for a change, Chase excitedly took the back stairs in one leap.

Throwing open the kitchen door he called out to her, "Kate. I'm back. And do I have something to tell…"

When he rounded the corner, he realized at once that Kate was not in the kitchen. Shelby was at the stove and Maddie sat in a high chair watching him intently.

"Well, hello, Chase. We weren't expecting you. Sorry. If you'd called to let us know, then…"

"Where is she, Shelby?" He steeled his expression so the disappointment wouldn't show.

"Uh…" Shelby looked nervous and it was suddenly driving him nuts.

"Is she okay?" he demanded. "She's not sick or anything?"

Shelby caught the panic in his voice. "Calm down. Kate's fine. The baby is fine. She just had a checkup this morning, and the doctor says all is well."

"Well then, where is she? Why isn't she here?"

"She's working."

"Excuse me? Working where?"

"She's been helping Robert Guidry over at the road-house tavern during happy hour. He needed the help and she felt she needed the extra money."

"What?" His ears were ringing. He could not have just heard that the love of his life, the soon-to-be-mother of his child was a barmaid.

"She doesn't need money," he argued. "All she has to do is ask me…."

Shelby laid a soft hand against his sleeve. "That's just it, Chase. She wanted some of her own, and she definitely didn't want to ask."

"Damned stubborn woman," he said as he stepped away from Shelby and headed for the Jag.

By the time he arrived at the tavern, Chase had calmed down. He had been so consumed over the last few weeks with his project that he had neglected the time with Kate that she obviously needed.

He'd been so sure of her capabilities to take care of herself and everyone around her. He'd just assumed she would think like he did and they wouldn't need to talk about every little detail. What an idiot he was.

Parking the car in the almost empty lot, Chase got out

and took a deep breath. She was her own woman. And thank heaven for her.

But he swore on his mother's grave that this was the last night she would ever work for anyone else.

He opened the tavern door and spotted her behind the bar. Just the sight of Kate made his knees weak and his pulse jump.

Happy hour had been over for a quarter hour and most of the patrons had gone on home. Kate stopped wiping down the bar and glanced up when the light in the room changed, meaning the outside door had opened. The bright lights from the parking lot flooded the entryway and she had to squint to see who had just come in.

And her heart leaped into her throat. Chase.

"Hey there, Guidry," he called out to Robert, who was at the other end of the bar. "I see you got yourself new help." Chase hadn't spoken directly to her, but he trained his eyes on her alone as he came closer.

"*Cher,* I…" she hesitated, not knowing what to say. Ecstatic to see him at last, she wanted to jump the bar and fling herself into his arms. But his face was a guarded mask. She couldn't tell what he was thinking.

Chase continued speaking to the bar owner as he climbed onto a bar stool right in front of where she stood. "You're going to have to find yourself someone else, Guidry. This barmaid is a short-timer. In fact, I'd say she has about five more minutes left."

Her anger came fast and hard. How dare he?

"Just a minute, Chase," she said with a frown.

He stunned her by grabbing her hands with both of his. "No, Kate," he said with a grin. "No more minutes left before I say what should've been said weeks ago. *Je t'aime.* I've never stopped loving you. Not for one single minute since the day I first saw you."

He pulled a small box from his jacket pocket. He flipped it open and turned the whole box around so she could see what it held.

She couldn't stop the gasp that escaped her lips. One of the biggest diamonds shone from the most fabulous ring setting she had ever beheld.

"Please do me the honor of becoming my wife."

Glancing from the ring back up into his eyes, Kate saw the emotion there that she had longed to see. He still loved her. For real.

Heart fluttering, she managed a grin of her own. "Yes, Chase. I will marry you."

He slipped the ring on her finger and leaned over the bar for a kiss. It was the tenderest of kisses. One of the sensual and endearing kinds, unlike any in her experience. Gentle, raw and full of every emotion that was running through them both, the kiss sent tears to her eyes. She pulled away, sniffed and held her hand, palm out, to study the ring.

Chase chuckled. And Robert whistled.

"That's some rock, Severin." Robert came closer to get a better look. "It's a wondrous thing to be seeing a Beltrane and a Severin about to be joined after all these generations. I guess that will surely be taking the curse off some folks round here."

"Curse?" both Chase and Kate asked at the same time.

Old Robert Guidry winked at them. "I told you I had some interesting history yet to tell, Severin. You ready to hear it?"

A superstitious curse wasn't particularly interesting to Chase. But it made him wonder if the old man might have the answers to any of the questions that still rumbled around in the back of his brain.

"Okay, Guidry. I'm listening." Chase eased back on his bar stool but took hold of Kate's hand across the mahogany bar. "*We're* listening. Go ahead with history."

The older man showed his yellowed teeth through a half smile. "Well now… It all started with your great-great-granddaddy Severin."

"Mine? Really?" Chase knew absolutely nothing about his family history—on either side.

"Jacques was his name," Guidry began. "Came down to bayou country to run the St. Germaine farm."

"Oh, yes," Kate murmured as she turned to Chase. "You remember. Gus told us that."

He nodded but kept silent, waiting for the rest.

"Your ancestor, son," Guidry continued. "He was a gambling man like you. Spent his spare time in barns and back rooms betting on games of chance.

"More than once he faced a young Beltrane boy name of Armand over cards and dice," Robert continued. "They had themselves a real rivalry going. Wanted the same land. Same women. Fought over everything."

Chase was feeling strange. This was not the story he'd been expecting to hear.

"One night a gypsy troop came to town," Robert told them as he picked up the bar towel and wiped his hands.

"Gypsies? You're kidding?"

"Wasn't so unusual back then. They came to small towns to sharpen knives, tell fortunes and part the locals from whatever they had that wasn't nailed down.

"Both of your ancestors fell in lust with the same gypsy woman," Robert said with a shake of his head. "She played them both for a while, then unfortunately fell hard for Jacques. Armand couldn't stand losing. It drove him mad. He went looking for them."

"Oh, dear," Kate said. "I'm not sure I want to hear the rest of this."

Robert patted her on the shoulder. "When the smoke cleared, both Armand and the gypsy woman were dead. Jacques was near death, too, but he pulled through.

"The gypsy woman's father was inconsolable," Robert told them as the story wound down. "He cursed both families. Swore they would pay for his daughter's death for generations."

"Okay," Chase interrupted when Robert took a breath. "That's enough about curses." He didn't like the horrified look on Kate's face. And the gypsy coincidence was just plain spooky.

Robert took the hint and put his arm around Kate's shoulders. "If there was a curse, Missy Kate, it ended with your father's death. Don't you worry about it."

Chase rolled his eyes over the fantasy tale about a curse. But there were other things he still wanted to know. He wondered if Robert Guidry would have the answers.

"Please don't try to tell me it was a family curse that drove Kate's father to hate me. That doesn't make…"

"You're right about that, son," Robert said. "Henry Beltrane had his very own evil spirits."

"Can you tell me about him?" Chase asked, but then thought better of it and turned to Kate. "You don't have to listen to this if you don't want to, *chère.*"

She seemed stronger now and shook her head. "I want to know whatever you can tell us about my father. I never understood the things he did."

Robert studied her through narrowed eyes for a few moments. "I suppose y'all both should be hearing the truth. Let the past be the past.

"Your father was a weak man, Kate," Robert continued in a bolder tone. "He was a spoiled-rotten boy that grew into a weak and selfish adult."

Chase decided Kate needed to sit down for this. "Come around the bar and sit with me, *chère*. I need you."

She lifted her chin as if to accuse him of trying to protect her—which of course he was. But he tried a smile and she smiled back. Then she came around the bar, climbed on a stool and he jumped up to stand behind her. He put his arms around her as she leaned against his chest for support. Her body was warm, and her strength washed right inside him.

It occurred to him then that he did need her. Much more than she needed him.

Guidry began his tale. "Henry Beltrane and Charles Severin went to school together and competed in everything. But it wasn't a fair competition. Sorry, Kate, but Henry was a born loser."

She nodded her head and made a motion with her hands for him to continue.

"Charles won the class president's job. He dated the prettiest girls. And though he couldn't take the time to participate in sports, whenever they faced each other in a game, Charles's team always won.

"Your daddy grew more hateful and bitter toward Charles every year," Robert continued with a sigh. "At their senior prom, Henry drank too much and pawed his date…tore her dress. Charles stepped in like the Southern gentlemen he was raised to be and took the scared girl home. Henry got himself a permanent mad-on cause of that, and swore then that he would someday get the better of Charles Severin."

"That sounds like my father," Kate told them. "But what happened to Charles to change him so much?"

Robert Guidry shook his head sadly. "The day Chase's mama was buried Charles picked up a bottle to drown his sorrows and just never could put it down again. And Henry Beltrane laughed in his face every day. Called him a ridiculous drunk.

"Your daddy used every nasty trick he knew to keep Charles Severin tied to that bottle, Kate," Robert told her darkly. "And it worked, too, until Chase finally rescued Charles and dried him out."

Kate twisted her head to question Chase. "You came here five years ago to save your father?"

Chase could only nod. Hearing that story had been difficult. Everything he'd ever imagined about his father was untrue. Chase's whole world seemed to be shifting.

"I wish I'd known you'd come home then," Kate said softly. "I might've…"

He looked down into the face of the woman he loved and saw great sorrow in her eyes. She was suffering from the sins of her father again. And Chase wouldn't stand for it.

He'd wanted his homecoming tonight to be a celebration. He'd wanted festive, not depressing. It was time to get them both out of here.

"Let's go, *chère*," he broke in before she could finish. "I have something good to tell you…in private."

Robert beamed at them both. "Anything you say will stay here, son."

"No chance, old man. You'll get the gossip soon enough. My fiancée hears the news first."

He shuttled them both out of the tavern and into the car. Dying to see Kate's expression change for the better, Chase couldn't wait to tell her how they were about to take the ultimate revenge.

"I thought you said your news was going to be good." Kate stared up at the moonlit outline of the old rice mill and shuddered. "Why did you bring me here? These ghostly walls are a far cry from anything pleasant. I thought we'd put the mill behind us forever."

Chase shifted the Jag into park and turned off the key. But he didn't make any attempt to get out of the car. Kate was really puzzled by his silence.

Finally he turned to her. "Do you remember what you said about the mill when we were on our way back from Gus's? About how it wasn't the mill itself that you were sorry to see fail. But that the loss of the town's jobs was going to be the real tragedy."

"Sure. I meant it, too. It's a shame. I hate that I let everyone down."

Chase ripped open his seat belt so he could put a hand on her shoulder. "You didn't. It was all your father's doing. He could never admit his failure, not even in order to save the mill and the town. After he drove it beyond redemption, you didn't stand a chance to succeed."

She took comfort from the heat of his hand on her

shoulder but wished they could go home. Increasingly desperate to get him back in her bed, his nearness had begun to cause other kinds of heat in her body.

"Can we talk about your good news now?" Kate urged.

He smiled at her, and his eyes crinkled with the surprise he was about to tell. "I'm sure I haven't missed anything where you're concerned. For instance, you'd be willing to work harder than ever in order to bring back the jobs that were lost. Am I right?"

She tilted her head to study his expression but couldn't get a handle on the meaning of his words. "Yes…of course, but…"

Chase flipped open her seat belt and helped her across the bucket-seat divide and into his lap. "That's better," he said with a grin.

Kate thought so, too. "Please tell me what's going on."

"It came to me easy as could be, Kate. The way to take the ultimate revenge against your father would be to build something useful on the site of his greatest failure."

Her breath caught in her throat. Was he saying what she thought he was saying?

"It took me three weeks of twenty-four-hour days and more money spent on lawyers than I'd thought possible. But I did it, Kate. I just got the final state approvals today.

"Next week we can start hiring construction crews to transform this hulk of a ghost mill into a four-star resort." He'd said it with a cat-who-ate-the-canary grin. "Within six months, the riverboat casino I special ordered will arrive for its permanent home at the old mill's dock."

She opened her mouth, but no words came out.

Chase laughed at her stunned expression. "I thought

we could discuss turning Live Oak Hall into a luxury spa to go with the resort. It won't take many changes on the inside. We'll definitely need to keep all your family's antiques."

Her head was spinning. "Wait… Let me catch my breath. You're saying you plan to turn the mill into a gambling casino and resort. And that such a thing will bring jobs back to the town." She blinked her eyes. "You intend to hire people from nearby?"

"Of course, *chère*." Chase laughed again at her confusion. "Actually, I've been thinking maybe Shelby might like a chance to manage her own restaurant. We'll need several nice places in the resort. I'll give her the job of food and beverage manager if she'd rather but…"

Kate actually heard a little-girl's squeal coming from her own mouth. She threw her arms around his neck and laughed out loud.

"It's so wonderful," she told him. "But what about your other businesses? Don't they need you, too? How will you ever be able to see this project through to the end?"

He wrapped her in his arms and lowered his voice. "Well, first of all, I'll have you to be the most competent partner a man could ever have. And secondly, most of my former businesses are already in escrow. The others are just waiting for higher bids."

She pulled back to look at him again. "You're selling all your businesses?"

He nuzzled her ear. "A family man needs to settle down, *chère*." His voice became husky with emotion. "Build a home. Become part of the community. Neither of our fathers managed to do that, and it caused a lot of hardship. I intend to see things change now."

Her heart was pounding so hard that she could barely hear his words. She pulled his head down so that their lips met and kissed him. Kissed him with every emotion she was still afraid to speak aloud.

It was all too exciting and wonderful. Her longtime dreams were coming true. But in her heart she had not forgotten that she didn't deserve this happiness. As much as she loved him and as wonderful as he had been, Kate was positive that he would go back to hating her and probably abandon her once more if he knew the whole truth.

The cold fear of losing him stole into her soul.

So she tried to bury her guilt for good. Maybe she could just forget it. Bury the truth so deeply that it never came to the surface.

Their kiss deepened, exploded into flames as each of them became consumed with the fire of desire. Time for talking had ended, and it soon became the time for showing…driving…taking…enveloping each other with hot, intense sensations.

Chase's mouth moved over hers. He claimed, bewitched, seduced. There was so much pleasure. So much promise.

Kate groaned, ground her bottom against his straining erection and reached to unbutton his shirt. She wanted to press her hands against his skin. To feel the smooth contours of muscle. To run her fingers through the silk of matted hair on his chest.

In one surprise sweep of his hands, Chase pulled her top up and over her head. Her breasts began to ache for his touch. When he bent his head to suckle a nipple with his hot mouth, Kate thought she might lose her mind.

She'd never before wanted him with such desperation. He was her hero and her lover. Her everything. For now. And she prayed that later would never come.

# Twelve

"No. No. No," Passionata Chagari screamed as she shook her fist at the darkness. "Of all the arrogant and smug young men. How dare you ignore the magic and close your eyes to the truth, Severin?"

In a fit of anger the old gypsy threw her crystal down on the swampy bog.

"You think you deserve this happiness and more?" she demanded of his shadow from afar. "You deserve nothing. Deep down, you really believe you were the only one wronged. Imagine that. And worse yet, now you think you've ridden in on your white horse to save the town by selfless acts?

"Damn you!" she continued, shrieking toward the shadows. "I gave my word that you would receive your heart's desire. You think this has all been good luck? Bah! Your heart's desire was to be loved. But no one deserves love until they can open their own heart. And you will receive nothing until you accept the truth."

Passionata paced under the willow and fumed. "You tell yourself you haven't missed anything where the woman is concerned," the gypsy mumbled angrily to herself. "Severin, you fool! You say you *love* her? Idiot! You crave her. That is not nearly good enough.

"No," she repeated aloud. "You are on the wrong path."

The old gypsy woman needed a better plan. She had given her word. Her ancestors expected the right result.

Passionata struggled to find the way. Her heart had already gone out to the woman. That would be where the answer was to be found, she was sure.

In a flash of thunder and magic, the correct answer came to her then. She saw the proper way at last.

Picking up her crystal, Passionata waved her arm out toward the old plantation. The magic was in the wrong hands.

It was time to set things to rights.

Chase's mind was reeling and his heart aching, as he leaned his forehead against the locked door and tried one last time. "Please tell me what's wrong, Kate. I don't understand."

Things between them had been deteriorating for the last ten days, since she'd agreed to the marriage. He had believed their problems were due to the onset of Kate's bouts with morning sickness. Chase was sure he would've had a rough time being happy and contented while living with anything as bad as that.

They were supposed to be married tomorrow, but

something else was wrong. Very wrong. And she wouldn't talk to him about it.

"Go away, Chase," she called out through the closed door. "It's over. We're not getting married tomorrow."

"Stop saying that and talk to me," he begged. But his pleas were met with silence, the same as they had been for the last hour.

Rubbing a hand over his jaw, Chase felt bruised. It was almost as if she had actually slapped him.

He didn't get it. What could possibly be so wrong?

Her sickness was only temporary. The doctor said so.

The construction on the outside of the house and on the mill appeared to be progressing too slowly, but still not that far off track. The town seemed genuinely pleased about changing from a mill town to a tourist destination. Their world was good.

Chase was so close to getting everything he had ever wanted that he could just taste it. But none of it would mean a thing without Kate. She was the key to his acceptance on the right side of town. Money and power meant nothing without her.

Without her? Oh God. How could she turn her back on him? Even though she had never told him she'd loved him, he knew she did. They shared a history. They would be sharing parenting duties for their child. And they were more than compatible in each other's arms.

That last thought took him to a place where erotic longings and staggering needs threatened to bring him to tears. She couldn't turn away from what they shared. It wasn't fair and would kill him.

Frustrated and hurting, Chase decided to try another route to discovering the answers. He headed down the stairs to find Shelby. If anyone would know Kate's heart, she would.

As usual, he found Shelby in the kitchen. He'd bought brand-new professional appliances for her to use, and all the stainless steel gleamed under the newly replaced lighting.

But Shelby wasn't cooking this afternoon. She was sitting at the long kitchen table working on the new laptop she'd bought after her last catering job. Maddie was napping beside her in a portable playpen.

Shelby looked up when he entered the room. "Is Kate okay? She told me to stop working on the reception and to begin contacting the guests to say the wedding's off. But I…"

"Don't," he said. "Not just yet, anyway."

He joined Shelby at the table. "Kate won't talk to me," he confessed. "I don't know if she's okay. I don't know what's wrong. Did something happen this morning that would've brought this on?"

Shelby shrugged one shoulder. "It didn't seem like much at the time, but I guess it must've affected Kate deeply. She's been getting more and more weepy every day. I thought it was just her raging hormones and the nausea. But this, well…"

"What?"

"Kate went down to the bayou at the edge of Live Oak property to collect Queen Anne's lace for the centerpieces. I'd told her we could order some from the florist in New Iberia, but she wouldn't hear of it."

Chase nodded. That did sound like Kate, but so what?

"She came back in a little while without any flowers. Her face was drained of all color, and her hands were shaking and cold. She looked scared to death."

"Why?" he interrupted. "What happened?" He would kill anyone or destroy anything that would upset her this way.

"I asked. She didn't want to talk about it. I finally got her to say she'd seen a swamp ghost, but then she said something like 'It was all her fault.'"

"A swamp ghost? That's just an old superstition. Was she hysterical or something?"

"No. She wasn't even crying at the time. I asked her what this ghost looked like and she said it was the gypsy…and then she mumbled something about a curse."

"The gypsy? Crap." He couldn't believe that the woman he loved, who usually seemed so in control and smart, would let her imagination run away with her like that. It had only been a fanciful story. Hadn't it?

"Do you know what she was talking about?"

"Maybe." He stood and squared his shoulders. "Can you tell me exactly where Kate was when she saw this gypsy? If I go there, perhaps I'll prove she was seeing swamp gas. Then I can convince her it was just a coincidence."

Shelby told him what she could about where the Queen Anne's lace grew. He stormed out of the house determined to make this right. His life would not be derailed by any old gypsy curse.

When he spotted the Queen Anne's lace growing next to the swamp, he thought he had the mystery solved. Sure enough, eerie green swamp gas was rising from the coffee-colored water.

The mist swirled around his ankles, and Chase couldn't help but wonder how a woman like Kate, who had been raised in bayou country, could make such a mistake. He'd known Guidry's tale had upset her, but this was carrying things too far.

As he peered out over the bog, Chase caught sight of something bright. Whatever it was, it seemed to be wavering in and out of view. Aha. Perhaps this would be what Kate had seen that frightened her into believing she'd seen a gypsy ghost.

He picked his way closer to the ancient willow where he'd spotted the object. When he got closer, he saw that it was a deep-purple and bright-red silk scarf, caught on a limb and waving like a flag in the wind.

However, somewhere way in the back of his mind, he knew there was no wind.

At first, Chase was really delighted with his find. He could take the scarf back and prove to Kate that she had not seen a ghost. But when he reached out and touched it, things changed.

Delight turned to confusion, and fear crept around the edges of his mind like the ghostly mist surrounding his body.

He'd seen this same scarf once before—on the old gypsy who'd given him the lucky egg. Chase's mind suddenly began to imagine strange things. He tried to ignore the odd sensation in his chest and the sudden ache in his temple.

But as if blinded by desire, Kate's face became all that he could see. Weird ideas popped into his mind unbidden.

No wonder Kate had been so unhappy, he thought absently. He hadn't given her a wedding gift yet.

Well, he could fix that right now. Without a second's hesitation, he reached into his pocket for the golden egg. Kate needed this much more than he did.

Pleased that he'd had such a fine idea for a gift, Chase stuffed the wildly colored scarf into his pocket, fisted his hand around the egg and headed back to the house. Smiling to himself, he just knew that soon everything would be as it should be.

Kate wasn't sure why she'd opened the door to Chase. But the sound of his voice when he'd come back upstairs had changed. Before he had sounded confused and annoyed. Now his voice was smooth and certain. She'd been intrigued to find out what had changed him.

Before she could ask, Chase pulled her into his arms and crushed his mouth on hers. Oh no, she begged him silently. Don't fog my mind, my love. I have to stay strong to save you.

He raised his head to take a breath and she pulled away. "What do you want, Chase? I'm not going to change my mind if that's what you think."

"I have something for you, *chère*. Please, let's sit down."

There wasn't anywhere to sit in this guest bedroom, save for the bed. And that seemed like taking a big chance.

But he slid his arm around her waist and pulled her down beside him on the edge of the bed. "Are you feeling well now? You're not sick, are you?" he asked with great concern.

She shook her head but stayed quiet. There was no sense upsetting him again. She felt okay now, but Kate was positive her good health was only temporary.

When she'd seen the ghost of that old gypsy, Kate had finally figured it out. The curse was not over.

As much as she wanted to be a mother. As much as she vowed never to leave her child the way she'd been left. It was not destined to happen.

She would lose this child the same way as she'd lost the one before. It didn't matter that the doctor said she was fine. The sickness she was experiencing now was exactly the same as long ago.

It was happening all over again. Seeing the gypsy's ghost proved it. They were cursed.

Chase would be devastated. Kate knew *she* deserved to be miserable for hiding the whole truth. But he didn't deserve that kind of pain.

She'd been racking her brain to find a way to make him go away. To save him. Maybe she should be the one to leave. Perhaps she could disappear.

"Shelby told me about you seeing the gypsy in the swamp, Kate. I'm sorry you were frightened."

"I didn't… I wasn't…"

Chase interrupted her by taking her hand and placing a tender kiss against her palm. "I have a wedding gift for you." He put his lucky golden egg in her open hand.

"But that's yours. Your good luck charm. Your inheritance."

"I want you to have it. It will bring you good luck. Protect you from bad luck and old curses."

He closed her fingers around the egg. "Feel how warm it is? That's the good luck seeping into your body."

"It doesn't feel warm to me," she told him. Kate was curious about it, though. What was different about this egg?

She peeled her fingers off and proceeded to study the design and the jewels. "Well, that's interesting. You didn't tell me the egg opened up. What's inside?"

Chase looked puzzled. "It doesn't. At least, I've never known it did."

Feeling a little chill of anticipation, Kate twisted the egg and it popped open. Immediately soft music began to play.

"It's a music box," she said, though that was obvious.

Chase's expression clouded over as he stared down at the egg in her hand. Kate's attention suddenly had been captured by the familiar notes coming from the open egg.

The song was a lullaby and it swept into her soul. Something half-remembered tugged at her heart. Dry tears were forming in her eyes and clogging her throat.

A vague voice inside the music urged her to finally do the right thing. Kate found she could not refuse.

She felt possessed. But deep down she was glad to at last be facing the truth.

"I have something to tell you, Chase," she began. "Remember when I said that my father had somehow found out about us, and we had been fighting that last afternoon?"

He nodded but kept his eyes trained on the egg.

"It was me," she confessed. "I told him. I...I had just taken a pregnancy test and knew I was going to have your baby."

Chase looked up sharply. He simply stared at her.

"I planned on telling you about the baby that night. Really I did. But I never got the chance."

Pain shot into his heart. His brain fogged over. He couldn't breathe.

A picture came into the back of his mind of her looking up from underneath him and saying, *I have something important to tell you.*

Oh, hell. He'd always believed she'd planned to tell him she loved him that night. But now he knew different.

He wanted to hit something. "Whatever would possess you to tell your father before telling me?"

"I explained that before, Chase. I was young and petrified. I would've had to leave high school. You had just graduated. How were we to live and support a baby? I thought he would help us. Give you a good job at the mill. Pay for the doctors."

She dropped her chin so he couldn't see her eyes. "I should've known better," she mumbled. "He demanded that I get rid of it. Said a Severin-Beltrane child had no business in this world."

In a blind rage Chase gripped her shoulders. "You didn't?" he growled.

Kate's head whipped up and she glared at him. "I can't believe you would ask me such a thing."

She was right. He knew better. Knew her better.

He dropped his hands. "Then where is the child? My child. Did you give it away?"

Kate stood and turned her back to him for a moment. She seemed to be composing herself. When she turned around, she looked stricken and sick. He wanted to help her. Hold her. But he couldn't. He couldn't even help himself.

"When you left town, I cried for days. I was so lonely and scared. Then the morning sickness came and I panicked.

"I had to find you," she continued sadly. "To tell you.

To…make you help us. I borrowed some money from Robert Guidry and got on a bus."

"Guidry loaned you money?"

Kate nodded. "Five hundred dollars. It took me nearly eight years to repay him. But he was the only one I trusted. I knew he wouldn't ask me to explain why I needed to find you."

Something inside Chase was cracking. He felt as if he was breaking in two and both halves were rolling toward the edge of a dangerous cliff.

He didn't want to the hear the rest. Couldn't stand to hear it. But he was frozen in place. He could see the edge of that abyss coming up fast.

"I searched for you everywhere I could think of," Kate told him. "For almost three months. I…I was desperate. So desperate, I forgot to eat, sometimes for days at a time. And when I did eat, it was junk. I didn't have much money.

"Then there were the nights I slept curled up in an alleyway. But I couldn't find you anywhere."

No. He couldn't bear it. The image of his Kate scared and so alone out there in the dark bore a hole into his soul. Chase stood and paced away from her.

"What happened to the baby, Kate?" He had to get her to finish the story so he could breathe again.

"Oh, Chase. I'm so sorry. Our baby…our little girl died. It was all my fault. I should've taken better care. The emergency room in that hospital in New Orleans tried to save her. But it was too soon." Kate covered her face with her hands and sobbed. "It was all my fault. Everything was all my fault."

The back of Chase's head exploded in a flash of

truth. His whole body throbbed with the searing pain, it doubled him over and blinded him.

"Oh my God." His chest was constricting. He couldn't accept what she'd said. But he knew she would never lie.

*Someone please stop the pain,* he begged silently. No, he thought crazily, instead, make it hurt much worse. Make it so bad that he could forget everything else.

In a fit of agony, Chase went to the closed window and put his fist right through the glass. He had been such an ass. An arrogant, self-righteous bastard. He deserved to burn in hell and much worse for this.

"Chase! What..?" Kate came over, reaching for his bleeding hand. "You're cut. Let me help you."

Ignoring her, Chase collapsed to his knees. He grabbed her around the waist and buried his face in her belly. "I left you behind," he gasped through the pain. "And just walked away. I was so hurt that I didn't stop to think. I can't believe I just didn't think."

Chase wished he could roll up in a ball and disappear. "I should've been with you. I left you to face your father and the pain all alone. Forgive me."

"It's… I…" Her voice was tight with emotion.

All of a sudden something even more horrible occurred to him. "After…afterward you came back here. Why, Kate?" Chase dreaded hearing her answer. He tilted his head to look up at her and held his breath.

"It was pretty stupid of me, I guess," she told him with chagrin. "But I thought you might come back for me. And I wanted to be where you could easily find me."

His mouth dropped open but no words came out.

"Took me two years to finally get it in my head that

you weren't coming right back," she continued. "By then it was also clear that the town needed me as the one sane Beltrane, acting as a buffer between them and my father."

Ten long years she had suffered alone with that bastard Beltrane. His darling had lived a miserable existence, while he basked gleefully in his anger and self-pity.

The hurt and sorrow in his heart grew so bad now Chase thought dying would be a better option. But he refused to die. Dying meant he would have to leave her all alone, and that was never going to happen again. Never again.

He stood so he could see her face. "I don't deserve you, my love. But I beg you not to leave me." He swiped the back of his uncut hand across his eyes to clear the tears, trying to see her better. "If you can't love me…or marry me…I understand. But give me a chance to make it right."

She'd been staring at his bleeding hand, but she raised her chin to gaze up at him. "I do love you, Chase. I always have. I said we couldn't get married because I'm scared. Afraid for our baby. Afraid of the curse."

*She loved him.* It took him a minute to process the rest of her statement. When he did, he pulled her close.

"There is no curse, *chère,*" he whispered. "I swear it. And this time I won't let anything happen to either one of you. We will have this baby…and many more. It won't make up for the one we lost, but our family will be together and strong in our love."

Kate touched his face tentatively and gazed into his eyes. "But I saw the gypsy ghost."

"No," he said as he pulled the scarf from his pocket. "This is a *real* scarf. Feel it. You saw a live person, not a ghost. If there ever was a curse, it's over."

She took the scarf from him, ran it slowly through her fingers, then broke down. Sobbing, she clung to him.

Chase held her close and fought his own tears of joy. It was a miracle. It was magic. It was his heart's desire.

*The gypsy.* He didn't know why, but the old woman had saved his life. He vowed to someday find the real reason.

"Tell me again, *chère,*" he whispered against her hair.

Kate pulled back with a wet twinkle in her eyes, knowing exactly what he wanted to hear. "I love you, Chase Severin. I always have. And I always will."

# Epilogue

**P**assionata Chagari stood in the shadows of Blackwater Bayou and watched as the lost heir to the gypsy inheritance married his heart's desire.

At last, she thought. Chase Severin had finally received his bequest. He'd become worthy of love.

She knew there was one more thing this particular heir would need to make her task complete, though. So when the wedding party congregated on the terrace for the reception, Passionata turned her thoughts toward making him aware of her presence. He deserved his answers.

Chase caught a glimpse of wild colors, flashing like a neon banner through the swamp brush. He made sure Kate was okay and occupied, then stole away and headed out.

He didn't have to search for long. The old gypsy that had given him the egg stood waiting for him under a willow.

"Tell me why you're here," he demanded. This was just plain creepy, and he hoped Kate wouldn't catch sight of her.

Passionata lifted her lips in a toothless grin. "You want one more story, Severin. I'm here to tell the tale."

He folded his arms across his chest. "Go ahead. But I don't believe in gypsy curses."

"You believe in the magic now, though, don't you?"

Chase had admitted to himself that his egg was truly magical, but he'd be damned if he would tell her that. "Just tell your story, old woman. What did my grandmother do that deserved such a legacy?"

She wasted no time in the telling. "In days gone by, gypsy troops were looked upon with distrust and distaste…perhaps we still are," she admitted. "When I was a young woman and round with my first child, something went terribly wrong. This was in the time before my father had found the magic. He wisely decided that my child and I needed a medical doctor since nothing else had worked.

"But none would attend me," the gypsy continued with a sad shake of her head. "My unborn child and I were mere hours away from leaving this earth when Lucille, herself a young girl at the time, found me, sneaked me into her father's mansion and begged her own doctor to come to my aide."

Chase was fascinated. But her tale seemed a little too close to his and Kate's story of a lost child. He rubbed his arms to stem an unusual and sudden chill.

"Without Lucille's kindness, my child and I would not have survived." The gypsy scowled at her memories. "For many years my father searched for a way of repayment. But Lucille seemed to need nothing we could give. Shortly before my father's death, he finally captured the magic…"

"Wait a sec," Chase interrupted. "How do you do that, exactly?"

Passionata waved his question away. "It is for gypsy ears alone, Severin. Ask not.

"The one thing Lucille wanted," she continued, "was a reunion with her only daughter, but that was beyond my father's power to grant by then. Her daughter, your mother, had died years earlier."

The gypsy's eyes grew watery with unshed tears. "My father was on his deathbed when he learned Lucille was nearing the end of her own time. So he fashioned his legacy and made me swear to fulfill it.

"I took his charge gladly as I too owed the debt," she continued. "The young Steele descendants were to receive a magical gift designed just for them. The bequests had been made to bring them love. The one thing each lacked but desired above all else."

She leaned back on her heels and folded her own arms over her chest in a mimicry of his. "And so it has been done."

It was an odd story, but Chase believed every word. He'd seen the magic work with his own eyes.

"I didn't search you out to hear your story, old woman. But I'm glad you told it."

Passionata tilted her head to question his motives.

Chase smiled at her. His life was filled with such love and happiness that he felt he would forever keep smiling.

"I came to give my thanks," he told her with a chuckle. "You saved my life with your magic, gypsy woman. Consider your obligation paid in full."

He turned away then, eager to return to his new wife. But he would always be grateful to a grandmother he had never known. And to a gypsy king that had captured the magic.

Life was good at last. And as long as Chase kept the love in his heart, it would always be magical.

* * * * *

# ✒ Silhouette®

# Desire.

**Coming in November
from Silhouette Desire**

# DYNASTIES: THE ASHTONS

*A family built on lies...brought together
by dark, passionate secrets*

**continues with**

# SAVOR THE SEDUCTION

## by Laura Wright

Grant Ashton came
to Napa Valley to discover the truth
about his family...but found so much
more. Was Anna Sheridan, a woman
battling her own demons, the answer
to all Grant's desires?

*Available this November wherever
Silhouette books are sold.*

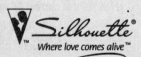

# Starting over is sweeter when shared.

What else could editor Elisha Reed do when
she suddenly goes from single workaholic
to mother of two teens?

# Starting from Scratch
## *Marie* Ferrarella

# Silhouette® Desire®

A new drama unfolds for
six of the state's wealthiest bachelors.

## THE SECRET DIARY

This newest installment continues with

# Highly Compromised Position

## by Sara Orwig

### (Silhouette Desire, #1689)

Rose Windcroft spent one incredible night with a
stranger…and now she's pregnant. But that's not the
worst part. The father of her child is none other than
Tom Devlin—a man whose family has been feuding
with her for years—and he's insisting on
revisiting that night!

*Available November 2005
at your favorite retail outlet.*

# Silhouette® Desire

## COMING NEXT MONTH

**#1687 SAVOR THE SEDUCTION—Laura Wright**
*Dynasties: The Ashtons*
Scandals had rocked his family but only one woman was able to shake him to the core.

**#1688 BOSS MAN—Diana Palmer**
*Long, Tall Texans*
This tough-as-leather attorney never looked twice at his dedicated assistant…until now!

**#1689 HIGHLY COMPROMISED POSITION—Sara Orwig**
*Texas Cattleman's Club: The Secret Diary*
How could she have known the sexy stranger who fathered her child was her family's sworn enemy?

**#1690 THE CHASE IS ON—Brenda Jackson**
*The Westmorelands*
His lovely new neighbor was a sweet temptation this confirmed bachelor couldn't resist.

**#1691 THE RUTHLESS GROOM—Bronwyn Jameson**
*Princes of the Outback*
She delivered the news that his bride-to-be had run away…never expecting to be next on his "to wed" list.

**#1692 MISTLETOE MANEUVERS—Margaret Alison**
Mixing business with pleasure could only lead to a hostile takeover…and a whole lot of passion.

SDCNM1005